# THE THUNDERBOLT

# The Thunderbolt

## An Episode in the History Of a Provincial Family

### In Four Acts

By
ARTHUR W. PINERO

BOSTON
WALTER H. BAKER & CO.

LONDON
WILLIAM HEINEMANN
MCMIX

# The Thunderbolt

## PLEASE READ CAREFULLY

# The Thunderbolt

## THE PERSONS OF THE PLAY

JAMES MORTIMORE.
ANN, *his wife.*
STEPHEN MORTIMORE.
LOUISA, *his wife.*
THADDEUS MORTIMORE.
PHYLLIS, *his wife.*
JOYCE ⎱ *The Thaddeus Mortimores' children.*
CYRIL ⎰
COLONEL PONTING.
ROSE, *his wife, née Mortimore.*
HELEN THORNHILL.
THE REV. GEORGE TRIST.
MR. VALLANCE, *solicitor, of Singlehampton.*
MR. ELKIN, *solicitor, of Linchpool.*
MR. DENYER, *a house-agent.*
HEATH, *a man-servant.*
*A servant girl at Nelson Villas.*
*Two others at " Ivanhoe."*

*The scene of the First Act is laid at Linchpool, a city in the Midlands. The rest of the action takes place, a month later, in the town of Singlehampton.*

# The Thunderbolt

## THE FIRST ACT

*The scene represents a large, oblong room, situated on the
ground floor and furnished as a library. At the back,
facing the spectator, are three sash windows, slightly re-
cessed, with venetian blinds. There is a chair in each
recess. At the further end of the right-hand wall a
door opens from the hall, the remaining part of the wall
—that nearer to the audience—being occupied by a long
dwarf-bookcase. This bookcase finishes at each end with
a cupboard, and on the top of each cupboard stands a
lamp. The keys of the cupboards are in their locks.*
*On the left-hand side of the room, in the middle of the
wall, is a fireplace with a fender-stool before it, and on
either side of the fireplace there is a tall bookcase with
glazed doors. A high-backed armchair faces the fireplace at the further end. A smoking-table with the
usual accessories, a chair, and a settee stand at the nearer
end of the fireplace, a few feet from the wall.*
*Almost in the centre of the room, facing the spectator, there
is a big knee-hole writing-table with a lamp upon it.
On the further side of the table is a writing-chair.
Another chair stands beside the table.*
*On the right, near the dwarf-bookcase, there is a circular
library-table on which are strewn books, newspapers, and*

1

*magazines.   Round this table a settee and three chairs
are arranged.*
*The furniture and decorations, without exhibiting any
special refinement of taste, are rich and massive.*
*The venetian blinds are down and the room is in semi-
darkness.   What light there is proceeds from the bright
sunshine visible through the slats.*
*Seated about the room, as if waiting for somebody to arrive,
are* JAMES *and* ANN MORTIMORE, STEPHEN *and* LOUISA,
THADDEUS *and* PHYLLIS, *and* COLONEL PONTING *and*
ROSE.   *The ladies are wearing their hats and gloves.
Everybody is in the sort of black which people hurriedly
muster while regular mourning is in the making—in the
case of the* MORTIMORES, *the black being added to ap-
parel of a less sombre kind.   All speak in subdued
voices.*
[*Note : Throughout, " right " and " left " are the spec-
tators' right and left, not the actor's.*]

### ROSE.

[*A lady of forty-four, fashionably dressed and coiffured
and with a suspiciously blooming complexion—on the settee on the left, fanning herself.*]   Oh, the heat!   I'm
stifled.

### LOUISA.

[*On the right—forty-six, a spare, thin-voiced woman.*]
Mayn't we have a window open?

### ANN.

[*Beside the writing-table—a stolid, corpulent woman of
fifty.*]   I don't think we *ought* to have a window open.

### JAMES.

[*At the writing-table—a burly, thick-set man, a little*

*older than his wife, with iron-gray hair and beard and a crape band round his sleeve.*] Phew! Why not, mother?

ANN.

It isn't usual in a house of mourning—except in the room where the ——

PONTING.

[*In the armchair before the fireplace—fifty-five, short, stout, apoplectic.*] Rubbish! [*Dabbing his brow.*] I beg your pardon—it's like the Black Hole of Calcutta.

THADDEUS.

[*Rising from the settee on the right, where he is sitting with* PHYLLIS—*a meek, care-worn man of two-and-forty.*] Shall I open one a little way?

STEPHEN.

[*On the further side of the library-table—forty-nine, bald, stooping, with red rims to his eyes, wearing spectacles.*] Do, Tad.

    [THADDEUS *goes to the window on the right and opens it.*

THADDEUS.

[*From behind the venetian blind.*] Here's a fly.

JAMES.

[*Taking out his watch as he rises.*] That'll be Crake. Half-past eleven. He's in good time.

THADDEUS.

[*Looking into the street.*] It isn't Crake. It's a young fellow.

JAMES.

Young fellow?

THADDEUS.

[*Emerging.*] It's Crake's partner.

JAMES.

His partner?

STEPHEN.

Crake has sent Vallance.

JAMES.

What's he done that for? Why hasn't he come him-self? This young man doesn't know anything about our family.

ANN.

He'll know the law, James.

JAMES.

Oh, the law's clear enough, mother.

> [*After a short silence,* HEATH, *a middle-aged man-servant, appears, followed by* VALLANCE. VALLANCE *is a young man of about five-and-thirty.*

HEATH.

Mr. Vallance.

JAMES.

[*Advancing to* VALLANCE *as* HEATH *retires.*] Good-morning.

VALLANCE.

Good-morning. [*Inquiringly.*] Mr. Mortimore?

JAMES.

James Mortimore.

VALLANCE.

Mr. Crake had your telegram yesterday evening.

JAMES.

Yes, he answered it, telling us to expect him.

VALLANCE.

He's obliged to go to London on business. He's very sorry. He thought I'd better run through.

JAMES.

Oh, well—glad to see you. [*Introducing the others.*] My wife. My sister Rose—Mrs. Ponting. My sister-in-law, Mrs. Stephen Mortimore. My sister-in-law, Mrs. Thaddeus. My brother Stephen.

STEPHEN.

[*Rising.*] Mr. Vallance was pointed out to me at the Institute the other night. [*Shaking hands with* VALLANCE.] You left by the eight forty-seven?

VALLANCE.

Yes. I changed at Mirtlesfield.

JAMES.

Colonel Ponting—my brother-in-law. [PONTING, *who has risen, nods to* VALLANCE *and joins* ROSE.] My younger brother, Thaddeus.

THADDEUS.

[*Who has moved away to the left.*] How d'ye do?

JAMES.

[*Putting* VALLANCE *into the chair before the writing-table and switching on the light of the lamp.*] You sit yourself down there. [*To everybody.*] Who's to be spokesman?

STEPHEN.

[*Joining* LOUISA.] Oh, you explain matters, Jim.
[LOUISA *makes way for* STEPHEN, *transferring
herself to another chair so that her husband
may be nearer* VALLANCE.

JAMES.

[*To* PONTING.] Colonel?

PONTING.

[*Sitting by* ROSE.] Certainly; you do the talking,
Mortimore.

JAMES.

[*Sitting, in the middle of the room, astride a chair,
which he fetches from the window on the right.*] Well,
Mr. Vallance, the reason we wired you yesterday—wired
Mr. Crake, rather—asking him to meet us here this morning, is this. Something has happened here in Linchpool
which makes it necessary for us to obtain a little legal
assistance.

VALLANCE.

Yes?

JAMES.

Not that we anticipate legal difficulties, whichever way
the affair shapes. At the same time, we consider it ad-
visable that we should be represented by our own solicitor—a solicitor who has our interests at heart, and
nobody's interests but ours. [*Looking round.*] Isn't that
it?

STEPHEN.

We want our interests watched—our interests ex-
clusively.

PONTING.

Watched—that's it. I'm speaking for my wife, of course.

ROSE.

[*With a languid drawl.*] Yes, watched. We should like our interests watched.

JAMES.

[*To* VALLANCE.] These are the facts. I'll start with a bit of history. We Mortimores are one of the oldest, and, I'm bold enough to say, one of the most respected, families in Singlehampton. You're a newcomer to the town ; so I'm obliged to tell you things I shouldn't have to tell Crake, who's been the family's solicitor for years. Four generations of Mortimores—I'm not counting our youngsters, who make a fifth—four generations of Mortimores have been born in Singlehampton, and the majority of 'em have earned their daily bread there.

VALLANCE.

Indeed ?

JAMES.

Yes, sir, indeed. Now, then. [*Pointing to the writing-table.*] Writing-paper's in the middle drawer. [VALLANCE *takes a sheet of paper from the drawer and arranges it before him.*] My dear father and mother—both passed away—had five children, four sons and a daughter. I'm the second son ; then comes Stephen ; then Rose—Mrs. Colonel Ponting ; then Thaddeus. You see us all round you.

VALLANCE.

[*Selecting a pen.*] Five children, you said ?

JAMES.

Five.  The eldest of us was Ned—Edward ——

STEPHEN.

Edward Thomas Mortimore.

JAMES.

Edward cut himself adrift from Singlehampton six-and-twenty years ago.  He died at a quarter-past three yesterday morning.

STEPHEN.

Up-stairs.

JAMES.

We're in his house.

STEPHEN.

We lay him to rest in the cemetery here on Monday.

VALLANCE.

[*Sympathetically.*]  I was reading in the train, in one of the Linchpool papers ——

JAMES.

Oh, they've got it in all their papers.

VALLANCE.

Mr. Mortimore, the brewer?

JAMES.

The same.  Aye, he was a big man in Linchpool.

STEPHEN.

A very big man.

JAMES.

And, what's more, a very wealthy one; there's no

doubt about that. Well, we can't find a will, Mr. Vallance.

VALLANCE.

Really?

JAMES.

To all appearances, my brother's left no will—died intestate.

VALLANCE.

Unmarried?

JAMES.

Unmarried ; a bachelor. Now, then, sir—just to satisfy my good lady—in the event of no will cropping up, what becomes of my poor brother's property?

VALLANCE.

It depends upon what the estate consists of. As much of it as is real estate would go to the heir-at-law—in this instance, the eldest surviving brother.

PONTING.

[*Impatiently.*] Yes, yes; but it's all personal estate—personal estate, every bit of it.

JAMES.

[*To* VALLANCE.] The Colonel's right. It's personal estate entirely, so we gather. The Colonel and I were pumping Elkin's managing-clerk about it this morning.

VALLANCE.

Elkin?

JAMES.

Elkin, Son and Tullis.

STEPHEN.

Mr. Elkin has acted as my poor brother's solicitor for the last fifteen years.

JAMES.

And *he's* never made a will for Ned.

STEPHEN.

Nor heard my brother mention the existence of one.

JAMES.

[*To* VALLANCE.]  Well?  In the case of personal estate —— ?

VALLANCE.

In that case, equal division between next-of-kin.

JAMES.

That's us—me, and my brothers, and my sister?

VALLANCE.

Yes.

JAMES.

[*To* ANN.]  What did I tell you, Ann?  [*To the rest.*] What did I tell everybody?

> [STEPHEN *polishes his spectacles, and* PONTING *pulls at his moustache, vigorously.* ROSE, ANN, *and* LOUISA *resettle themselves in their seats with great contentment.*

VALLANCE.

[*Writing.*]  " Edward "—  [*looking up*]  Thomas? [JAMES *nods.*]  " Thomas—Mortimore ——"

JAMES.

Of 3 Cannon Row and Horton Lane ——

STEPHEN.

Horton Lane is where the brewery is.

JAMES.

Linchpool, brewer.

STEPHEN.

"Gentleman" is the more correct description. The business was converted into a company in nineteen-hundred-and-four.

LOUISA.

Gentleman, ah! What a gentlemanly man he was!

ANN.

A perfect gentleman in every respect.

ROSE.

Most gentlemanlike, poor dear thing.

PONTING.

Must have been. I never saw him—but must have been.

JAMES.

[*To* VALLANCE.] Gentleman, deceased ——

STEPHEN.

Died, June the twentieth ——

JAMES.

Aged fifty-three. Two years my senior.

VALLANCE.

[*With due mournfulness.*] No older? [*Writing.*] You are James ——

JAMES.

James Henry. "Ivanhoe," Claybrook Road, and Victoria Yard, Singlehampton, builder and contractor.

ANN.

My husband is a parish guardian and a rural-district councilman.

JAMES.

Never mind that, mother.

ANN.

Eight years treasurer of the Institute, and one of the founders of the Singlehampton and Claybrook Temperance League.

LOUISA.

Stephen was one of the founders of the League too—weren't you, Stephen ?

JAMES.

[*To* VALLANCE.] Stephen Philip Mortimore, 11 The Crescent, and 32 King Street, Singlehampton, printer and publisher; editor and proprietor of our Singlehampton *Times and Mirror*.

LOUISA.

Author of the History of Singlehampton and its Surroundings ——

STEPHEN.

All right, Lou.

LOUISA.

With Ordnance Map.

JAMES.

Rose Emily Rackstraw Ponting ——

ROSE.

My mother was a Rackstraw.

JAMES.

Wife of Arthur Everard Ponting, West Sussex Regiment, Colonel, retired, 17a Coningsby Place, South Belgravia, London. That's the lot.

ANN.

No ——

JAMES.

Oh, there's Tad. [*To* VALLANCE.] Thaddeus John Mortimore ——

THADDEUS.

[*Who is standing, looking on, with his elbows resting upon the back of the chair before the fireplace—smiling diffidently.*] Don't forget me, Jim.

JAMES.

6 Nelson Villas, Singlehampton, professor of music. Any further particulars, Mr. Vallance?

VALLANCE.

[*Finishing writing and leaning back in his chair.*] May I ask, Mr. Mortimore, what terms you and your sister and brothers were on with the late Mr. Mortimore?

JAMES.

Terms?

VALLANCE.

What I mean is, your late brother was a man of more than ordinary intelligence ; he must have known who his estate would benefit, in the event of his dying intestate.

JAMES.

[*With a nod.*]  Aye.

VALLANCE.

My point is, was he on such terms with you as to make it reasonably probable that he should have desired his estate to pass to those who are here ?

JAMES.

[*Rubbing his beard.*]  Reasonably probable ?

STEPHEN.

Certainly.

PONTING.

In my opinion, certainly.

JAMES.

[*Looking at the others.*]  He sent for us when he was near his end ——

STEPHEN.

Showing that old sores were healed—thoroughly healed —as far as he was concerned.

VALLANCE.

Old sores ?

JAMES.

He wouldn't have done that if he hadn't had a fondness for his family—eh ?

ANN.

Of course not.

LOUISA.

Of course he wouldn't.

PONTING.

Quite so.

VALLANCE.

Then, I take it, there had been—er——?

STEPHEN.

An estrangement.  Yes, there *had*.

JAMES.

Oh, I'm not one for keeping anything in the background.  Up to a day or two before his death, we hadn't been on what you'd call terms with my brother for many years, Mr. Vallance.

STEPHEN.

Unhappily.

JAMES.

*De mortuis*—how's it go——?

STEPHEN.

*De mortuis nil nisi bonum.*

JAMES.

Well, plain English is good enough for me.  [*To* VALLANCE.]  But I don't attempt to deny it—at one time of his life my poor brother Edward was a bit of a scamp, sir.

STEPHEN.

A little rackety—a little wild.  Young men will be young men.

ANN.

[*Shaking her head.*]  I've a grown-up son myself.

LOUISA.

[*Inconsequently.*] And there are two sides to every question.   I always say—don't I, Stephen——?

STEPHEN.

Yes, yes, yes.

LOUISA.

There are two sides to every question.

JAMES.

[*To* VALLANCE.] No, sir, after Edward cleared out of Singlehampton, we didn't see him again, any of us, till about fifteen years back.   Then he came to settle here, in this city, and bought Cordingly's brewery.

LOUISA.

Only forty miles away from his birthplace.

STEPHEN.

Forty-two miles.

LOUISA.

That was fate.

STEPHEN.

Chance.

LOUISA.

*I* don't know the difference between chance and fate.

STEPHEN.

[*Irritably.*] No, you don't, Lou.

JAMES.

Then some of us used to knock up against him occasionally—generally on the line, at Mirtlesfield junction. But it was only a nod, or a how-d'ye-do, we got from him ; and it never struck us till last Tuesday morning that he kept a soft corner in his heart for us all.

VALLANCE.

Tuesday ——?

ANN.

First post.

JAMES.

We had a letter from Elkin, telling us that poor Ned was seriously ill ; and saying that he was willing to shake hands with the principal members of the family, if they chose to come through to Linchpool.

STEPHEN.

Thank God we came.

JAMES.

Aye, thank God.

ANN *and* LOUISA.

Thank God.

ROSE.

[*Affectedly.*] It will always be a sorrow to me that I didn't get down till it was too late. I shall never cease to reproach myself.

JAMES.

[*Indulgently.*] Oh, well, you're a woman o' fashion, Rose.

ROSE.

[*With a simper.*] Still, if I had guessed the end was as near as it was, I'd have given up my social engagements without a murmur. [*Appealing to* PONTING.] Toby ——!

PONTING.

Without a murmur—without a murmur; both of us would.

VALLANCE.

[*Rising, putting his notes into his pocketbook as he speaks.*] I think it would perhaps be as well that I should meet Mr. Elkin.

STEPHEN.

That's the plan.

JAMES.

[*Rising.*] Just what I was going to propose.

STEPHEN.

Elkin knows we have communicated with our solicitor.

JAMES.

[*Looking at his watch.*] He's gone round to the Safe Deposit Company in Lemon Street.

STEPHEN.

His latest idea is that my brother may have rented a safe there.

PONTING.

[*Who has risen with* JAMES.] Preposterous. Never heard anything more grotesque.

JAMES.

The old gentleman will want to drag the river Linch next.

PONTING.

As if a man of wealth and position, with safes and strong-rooms of his own, would deposit his will in a place of that sort. 'Pon my word, it's outrageous of Elkin.

STEPHEN.

It does seem rather extravagant.

ROSE.

Absurd.

VALLANCE.

[*Coming forward.*] We must remember that it's the duty of all concerned to use every possible means of discovery. [*To* JAMES.] Your brother had an office at the brewery?

JAMES.

Elkin and I turned that inside-out yesterday.

STEPHEN.

In the presence of Mr. Holt and Mr. Friswell, two of the directors.

VALLANCE.

And his bank ——?

JAMES.

London City and Midland. Four tin boxes. We've been through 'em.

STEPHEN.

The most likely place of deposit, I should have thought, was the safe in this room.

PONTING.

Exactly. The will would have been there if there had been a will at all.

[JAMES *switches on the light of the lamp which stands above the cupboard at the further end of the dwarf-bookcase.*

JAMES.

[*Opening the cupboard and revealing a safe.*] Yes, this is where my brother's private papers are.

STEPHEN.

This was his library and sanctum.

JAMES.

[*Listening as he shuts the cupboard door.*] Hallo! [*Opening the room door a few inches and peering into the hall.*] Here *is* Elkin. [*There is a slight general movement denoting intense interest and suspense.* ANN *gets to her feet.* JAMES *closes the door and comes forward a little—grimly.*] Well! Hey! I wonder whether he's found anything in Lemon Street?

PONTING.

[*Clutching* ROSE'S *shoulder and dropping back into his chair—under his breath.*] Good God !

ANN.

[*Staring at her husband.*] James —— !

JAMES.

[*Sternly.*] Go and sit down, mother. [ANN *retreats and seats herself beside* ROSE.] If he *has*, we ought to feel glad ; that's how we ought to feel.

STEPHEN.

[*Resentfully.*] Of course we ought. That's how we *shall* feel.

JAMES.

Poor old Ned ! It's his wishes we've got to consider —[*returning to the door*] his wishes. [*Opening the door again.*] Come in, Mr. Elkin. Waiting for you, sir. [*He admits* ELKIN, *a gray-haired, elderly man of sixty. Pre-*

*sents* VALLANCE.] Mr. Vallance—Crake and Vallance, Singlehampton, our solicitors. [ELKIN *advances and shakes hands with* VALLANCE.] Mr. Vallance has just run over to see how we're getting on.

ELKIN.

[*To* VALLANCE, *genially.*] I don't go often to Single-hampton nowadays. I recollect the time, Mr. Vallance, when the whole of the south side of the town was meadow-land. Would you believe it—meadow-land! And where they've built the new hospital, old Dicky Dunn, the farmer, used to graze his cattle. [*To* JAMES, *who is touching his sleeve.*] Eh?

JAMES.

[*Rather huskily.*] Excuse me. Any luck?

ELKIN.

Luck?

JAMES.

In Lemon Street. Find anything?

ELKIN.

[*Shaking his head.*] No. There is nothing there in your brother's name. [*Again there is a general move-ment, but this time of relief.*] It was worth trying.

JAMES.

Oh, it was worth trying.

STEPHEN.

[*Heartily.*] Everything's worth trying.

PONTING.

[*Jumping up.*] Everything. Mustn't leave a stone unturned.

[*The strain being over,* ROSE *and* ANN *rise and
go to the fireplace, where* PONTING *joins them.*
THADDEUS *moves away and seats himself at
the centre window.*

ELKIN.

[*Sitting beside the writing-table.*] This is a puzzling
state of affairs, Mr. Vallance.

VALLANCE.

Oh, come, Mr. Elkin!

ELKIN.

I don't want to appear uncivil to these ladies and
gentlemen—very puzzling.

VALLANCE.

Scarcely what one would have expected, perhaps ; but
what is there that's puzzling about it ?

JAMES.

[*Standing by* ELKIN.] People have died intestate before to-day, Mr. Elkin.

STEPHEN.

It's a common enough occurrence.

VALLANCE.

[*To* ELKIN.] I understand you acted for the late Mr.
Mortimore for a great many years?

ELKIN.

Ever since he came to Linchpool.

·   VALLANCE.

His most prosperous years.

[ELKIN *assents silently.*

JAMES.

When he was making money to *leave.*

VALLANCE.

[*To* ELKIN.] And the subject of a will was never broached between you ?

ELKIN.

I won't say that. I've thrown out a hint or two at different times.

VALLANCE.

Without any response on his part ?

ELKIN.

Without any practical response, I admit. [JAMES *and* STEPHEN *shrug their shoulders.*] But he must have employed other solicitors previous to my connection with him. I can't trace his having done so ; but no commercial man gets to eight-and-thirty without having something to do with us chaps.

VALLANCE.

[*Sitting on the settee on the left.*] Assuming a will of long standing, he may have destroyed it, may he not, recently ?

ELKIN.

Recently ?

VALLANCE.

Quite recently. Here we have a man at variance with his family and dangerously ill. What do we find him doing ? We find him summoning his relatives to his bedside and becoming reconciled to them ——

JAMES.

Completely reconciled.

STEPHEN.

Completely.

ELKIN.

[*To* VALLANCE.]  At my persuasion.  I put pressure on him to send for his belongings.

VALLANCE.

Indeed?  Granting that, isn't it reasonable to suppose that, subsequent to this reconciliation ——?

ELKIN.

Oh, no : he destroyed no document of any description after he took to his bed.  That I've ascertained.

VALLANCE.

Well, theorizing is of no use, is it?  We have to deal with the simple fact, Mr. Elkin.

JAMES.

Yes, that's all we have to deal with.

STEPHEN.

The simple fact.

ELKIN.

No will.

PONTING.

[*Who, with the rest, has been following the conversation between* ELKIN *and* VALLANCE.]  No will.

ELKIN.

[*After a pause.*]  Do you know, Mr. Vallance, there is one thing I shouldn't have been unprepared for?

VALLANCE.

What?

ELKIN.

A will drawn by another solicitor, behind my back, *during* my association with Mr. Mortimore.

VALLANCE.

Behind your back?

ELKIN.

He was a most attractive creature—one of the most engaging and one of the ablest, I've ever come across ; but he was remarkably secretive with me in matters relating to his private affairs—remarkably secretive.

VALLANCE.

Secretive?

ELKIN.

Reserved, if you like. Why, it wasn't till a few days before his death—last Saturday—it wasn't till last Saturday that he first spoke to me about this child of his.

VALLANCE.

Child? '

ELKIN.

This young lady we are going to see presently.

VALLANCE.

[*Looking at* JAMES *and* STEPHEN.] Oh, I—I haven't heard anything of her.

ELKIN.

Bless me, haven't you been told?

JAMES.

[*Uncomfortably.*] We hadn't got as far as that with Mr. Vallance.

STEPHEN.

[*Clearing his throat.*] Mr. Elkin did not think fit to inform *us* of her existence till yesterday.

JAMES.

[*Looking at his watch.*] Twelve o'clock she's due, isn't she?

ELKIN.

[*To* JAMES.] You fixed the hour. [*To* VALLANCE.] I wrote to her at the same time that I communicated with his brothers. Unfortunately she was away, visiting.

STEPHEN.

She's studying painting at one of these art-schools in Paris.

ELKIN.

She arrived late last night. Mrs. Elkin and I received her. Only four-and-twenty. A nice girl.

VALLANCE.

Is the mother living?

ELKIN.

No.

JAMES.

The mother was a person of the name of Thornhill.

STEPHEN.

Calling herself Thornhill—some woman in London. She died when the child was quite small.

JAMES.

[*With a jerk of the head towards the safe.*] There's a bundle of the mother's letters in the safe.

ELKIN.

This meeting with the family is my arranging. As matters stand, Miss Thornhill is absolutely unprovided for, Mr. Vallance. And there was the utmost affection between Mr. Mortimore and his daughter—as he acknowledged her to be—undoubtedly. Now you won't grumble at me for my use of the word "puzzling"?

VALLANCE.

[*Looking round.*] I am sure my clients, should the responsibility ultimately rest with them, will do what is just and fitting with regard to the young lady.

JAMES.

More than just—more than just, if it's left to me.

STEPHEN.

We should be only too anxious to behave in a liberal manner, Mr. Vallance.

LOUISA.

We're parents ourselves—all except Colonel and Mrs. Ponting.

ANN.

My own girl—my Cissy—is nearly four-and-twenty.

ROSE.

[*Seated upon the fender-stool.*] I suppose we should have to make her an allowance of sorts, shouldn't we?

JAMES.

A monthly allowance.

STEPHEN.

Monthly or quarterly.

PONTING.

Yes, but this art-school in Paris—you've no conception
what that kind of fun runs into.

JAMES.

Schooling doesn't go on forever, Colonel.

PONTING.

But it'll lead to an *atelier*—a studio—if you're not
careful.

ROSE.

The art-school could be dropped, surely?

STEPHEN.

Perhaps the art-school isn't strictly necessary.

ROSE.

And she has an address in a most expensive quarter
of Paris—didn't you say, Jim?

JAMES.

The Colonel says it's a swell locality.

PONTING.

Most expensive.   The father—if he *was* her father—
seems to have squandered money on her.

STEPHEN.

Well, well, we shall see what's to be done.

PONTING.

Squandered money on her recklessly.

JAMES.

Yes, yes, we'll see, Colonel ; we'll see.

[PHYLLIS, *who has taken no part in what has been going on, suddenly rises. She is a woman of thirty-five, white-faced and faded, but with decided traces of beauty. Everybody looks at her in surprise.*

PHYLLIS.

[*Falteringly.*] I—I beg your pardon ——

LOUISA.

[*Startled.*] Good gracious me, Phyllis!

PHYLLIS.

[*Gaining firmness as she proceeds.*] I beg your pardon. With every respect for Rose and Colonel Ponting, if we come into Edward Mortimore's money, we mustn't let it make an atom of difference to the child.

LOUISA.

Really, Phyllis !

STEPHEN.

[*Stiffly.*] My dear Phyllis ——

JAMES.

[*Half amused, half contemptuously.*] Oh, we mustn't, mustn't we, Phyllis ?

PHYLLIS.

He was awfully devoted to her in his lifetime, it turns out. Colonel Ponting and Rose ought to remember that.

PONTING.

[*Walking away in umbrage to the window on the left, followed by* ROSE.] Thank you, Mrs. Thaddeus.

THADDEUS.
[*Who has risen and come to the writing-table.*] Phyl—
Phyl——

PHYLLIS.
[*To* JAMES *and* STEPHEN.] Jim—Stephen—you couldn't
stint the girl after pocketing your brother's money ; you
couldn't do it!

ANN.
James——

JAMES.
Eh, mother?

ANN.
I don't think we need to be taught our duty by
Phyllis.

STEPHEN.
[*Rising and going over to the fireplace.*] Frankly, I
don't think we need.

LOUISA.
[*Following him.*] Before Mr. Elkin and Mr. Vallance!

THADDEUS.
Stephen—Lou—you don't understand Phyl.

JAMES.
It isn't for want of plain speaking, Tad.

THADDEUS.
[*Sitting at the writing-table.*] No, but listen—Jim——

JAMES.
[*Joining those at the fireplace.*] Blessed if I've ever
been spoken to in this style in my life!

THADDEUS.

Jim, listen. If we come into Ned's money, we come into his debts into the bargain. There are no assets without liabilities. The girl's a debt—a big debt, as it were. Well, what does she cost? Five hundred a year? Six—seven—eight hundred a year? What's it matter? What would a thousand a year matter? Whatever Ned could afford, *we* could, amongst us. Why he should have neglected to make Miss Thornhill independent is a mystery—I'm with you there, Mr. Elkin. Perhaps his sending for us, and shaking hands with us as he did, was his way of giving her into our charge. Heaven knows what was in his mind. But this is certain—if it falls to our lot to administer to Ned's estate, we administer, not only to the money, but to the girl, and the art-school, and her comfortable lodgings, and anything else in reason. There's nothing offensive in our saying this.

ELKIN.

Not in the least.

THADDEUS.

[*With a deprecating little laugh.*] Ha! We don't often put our oar into family discussions, Phyl and I. Stephen—[*turning in his chair*] Rosie ——

JAMES.

[*Looking down on* THADDEUS—*grinning.*] Hallo, Tad! Why, I've always had the credit of being the speaker o' the family. You're developing all of a sudden.

[HEATH *enters.*

HEATH.

[*Looking round the room.*] Mrs. Thaddeus Mortimore ——?

THADDEUS.

[*Pointing to* PHYLLIS *who is now seated in a chair on the right.*] Here she is.

HEATH.

[*In a hushed voice.*] Two young ladies from Roper's, to fit Mrs. Thaddeus Mortimore with her mourning.

THADDEUS.

[*Rising.*] They weren't ready for Phyllis at ten o'clock. [*Over his shoulder, as he joins* PHYLLIS *at the door.*] Hope you don't object to their waiting on her here.

HEATH.

[*To* THADDEUS.] On the first floor, sir.
          [PHYLLIS *and* THADDEUS *go out.* HEATH *is following them.*

VALLANCE.

[*To* HEATH, *rising.*] Er—— [*To* ELKIN.] What's his name?

ELKIN.

[*Calling to* HEATH, *who returns.*] Heath ——

VALLANCE.

[*Going to* HEATH.] Have you a room where Mr. Elkin and I can be alone for a few minutes?

HEATH.

There's the dining-room, sir.

VALLANCE.

[*Turning to* ELKIN.] Shall we have a little talk together?

ELKIN.

[*Rising.*] By all means.

VALLANCE.

[*To the others.*] Will you excuse us?

ELKIN.

[*Taking* VALLANCE'S *arm.*] Come along. [*Passing out with* VALLANCE—*regretfully.*] Ah, Heath, the dining-room ——!

HEATH.

[*As he disappears, closing the door.*] Yes, Mr. Elkin ; that's over, sir.

JAMES.

[*Who has crossed over to the right, to watch the withdrawal of* ELKIN *and* VALLANCE.] What have those two got to say to each other on the quiet in such a deuce of a hurry ?

PONTING.

[*Coming forward.*] My dear good friends, I beg you won't think me too presuming ——

JAMES.

[*Sourly.*] What is it, Colonel?

PONTING.

But you mustn't, you really mustn't, allow yourselves to be dictated to—bullied ——

JAMES.

Bullied ?

PONTING.

Into doing anything that isn't perfectly agreeable to you.

STEPHEN.

You consider we're being bullied, Colonel ?

JAMES.

If it comes to bullying ——

PONTING.

It *has* come to bullying, if I'm any judge of bullying. First, you have Mr. Elkin, a meddlesome, obstructive ——

STEPHEN.

[*Sitting at the writing-table.*] Oh, he's obviously antagonistic to us—obviously.

PONTING.

Of course he is. He sniffs a little job of work over this Miss Thornhill. It's his policy to cram Miss Thornhill down our throats. That's his game.

JAMES.

[*Between his teeth.*] By George —— !

PONTING.

And then you get Mr. Vallance, your own lawyer ——

JAMES.

[*Sitting in a chair on the right.*] Aye, I'm a bit disappointed with Vallance.

PONTING.

Dogmatizing about what is just and what is fitting ——

STEPHEN.

Hear, hear, Colonel! You don't pay a solicitor to take sides against you.

JAMES.

As if we couldn't be trusted to do the fair thing of our own accord !

PONTING.

The upshot being that Miss Thornhill, supported openly by the one, and tacitly by the other, will be marching in here and—and——

JAMES.

Kicking up a rumpus.

PONTING.

I shouldn't be surprised.

LOUISA.

A rumpus! [*Sitting upon the settee on the left.*] She wouldn't dare.

ANN.

[*Rising.*] That would be terrible—a rumpus——

ROSE.

[*In the middle of the room.*] I shouldn't be surprised either. You mustn't expect too much, you know, from a girl who's——

STEPHEN.

[*Interpreting* ROSE'S *shrug.*] Illegitimate.

ANN.

No, I suppose we oughtn't to expect her to be the same as our children.

PONTING.

And finally, to cap it all, you have your brother Thaddeus—your brother——

JAMES.

Ha, yes! Tad obliged us with a pretty stiff lecture, didn't he?

LOUISA.

So did Phyllis.

ANN.

[*Seating herself beside* LOUISA.] It was Phyllis who began it.

ROSE.

[*Swaying herself to and fro upon the back of the chair next to the writing-table.*] Tad's wife! She's a suitable person to be lectured by, I must say.

STEPHEN.

Poor old Tad! He was only trying to excuse her rudeness.

ROSE.

Just fancy! The two Tads sharing equally with ourselves!

STEPHEN.

It *is* curious, at first sight.

ROSE.

Extraordinary.

STEPHEN.

But, naturally, the law makes no distinctions.

ROSE.

No. It was the lady's method of announcing that she's as good as we are.

JAMES.

Tad and his wife with forty or fifty thousand pound, p'r'aps, to play with! So the world wags.

ROSE.

Positively maddening.

LOUISA.

We shall see Phyllis aping us now more than ever.

ANN.

And making that boy and girl of hers still more conceited.

LOUISA.

They needn't let apartments any longer ; that's a mercy.

ANN.

We shall be spared that disgrace.

JAMES.

Strong language, mother !

STEPHEN.

Hardly disgrace. You can't call the curate of their parish church a lodger in the ordinary sense of the term.

LOUISA.

Phyllis's girl might make a match of it with Mr. Trist in a couple of years' time. She's fifteen.

ANN.

A forward fifteen.

ROSE.

It's a fairy story. A woman who's brought nothing but the worst of luck to Tad from the day he married her !

JAMES.

The devil's luck.

STEPHEN.

Been his ruin—his ruin professionally—without the shadow of a doubt.

LOUISA.

Such a good-looking fellow he used to be, too.

ANN.

Handsome.

LOUISA.

[*Archly.*] It was Tad I fell in love with, Stephen—not with you.

STEPHEN.

And popular. *He'd* have had the conductorship of the choral societies but for his mistake ; Rawlinson would never have had it.   Councillor Pritchard admitted as much at a committee-meeting.

PONTING.

[*Seated upon the settee on the right.*] Butcher—the wife's father—wasn't he ?

ROSE.

Just as bad.   Old Burdock kept a grocer's shop at the corner of East Street.

STEPHEN.

West Street.

ROSE.

West Street, was it ?   She's the common or garden over-educated petty-tradesman's daughter.

JAMES.

[*Oratorically.*]  No, no ; you can't *over* educate, Rose. You can *wrongly* educate ——

ROSE.

Oh, don't start that, Jim. [*To* PONTING.] She was a pupil of Tad's.

STEPHEN.

[*Holding up his hands.*] Marriage—marriage ——!

LOUISA.

Stephen !

JAMES.

If it isn't the right sort o' marriage —— !

STEPHEN.

Poor old Tad !

JAMES.

*Rich* old Tad to-day, though ! [*Chuckling.*] Ha, ha !

ROSE.

[*Glancing at the door.*] Sssh —— !
[THADDEUS *returns. The others look down their noses or at distant objects.*

THADDEUS.

[*Closing the door and advancing.*] I—I hope you're not angry with Phyllis.

STEPHEN.

[*Resignedly.*] Angry?

THADDEUS.

Or with me.

ANN.

Anger would be out of place in a house of mourning.

JAMES.

Women's tongues, Tad !

STEPHEN.

Yes ; the ladies—they will make mischief.

LOUISA.

Not every woman, Stephen.

THADDEUS.

Phyllis hasn't the slightest desire to make mischief.
Why on earth should Phyl want to make mischief?
[*Sitting in the chair in the middle of the room.*] She's a
little nervy—a little unstrung ; that's what's the matter
with Phyllis.

LOUISA.

There's no cause for *her* to be specially upset that I
can think of.

ANN.

*She* didn't know Edward in the old days as we did.

THADDEUS.

No, but being with him on Wednesday night, when the
change came—that's affected her very deeply, poor girl ;
bowled her over. [*To* ROSE.] She helped to nurse him.

ROSE.

[*Indifferently.*] One of the nurses cracked up, didn't
she ?

JAMES.

The night-nurse.

THADDEUS.

[*Nodding.*] Sent word late on Wednesday afternoon
that she couldn't attend to her duties.

STEPHEN.

The day-nurse knocking off at eight o'clock ! Dreadful !

THADDEUS.

There we were, rushing about all over the place—all over the place—to find a substitute.

JAMES.

And no success.

THADDEUS.

[*Rubbing his knees.*] There's where Phyllis came in handy ; there's where Phyl came in handy.

LOUISA.

Phyllis hadn't more than two or three hours of it, while Ann and I were resting, when all's said and done.

ANN.

Not more than two or three hours alone, at the outside.

THADDEUS.

No ; but, as I say, it was during those two or three hours that the change set in.   It's been a shock to her.

LOUISA.

The truth is, Phyllis delights in making a fuss, Tad.

THADDEUS.

Phyl !

ANN.

She loves to make a martyr of herself.

THADDEUS.

Phyl does !

LOUISA.

*You* delight to make a martyr of her, then ; perhaps that's it.

ANN.

I suppose you do it to hide her faults.

LOUISA.

It would be far more sensible of you, Tad, to strive to correct them ——

ANN.

If it's not too late—far more sensible.

LOUISA.

And teach her a different system of managing her home ——

ANN.

And how to bring up her children more in keeping with their position ——

LOUISA.

With less pride and display.

ANN.

They treat their *cousins* precisely like dirt.

LOUISA.

Dirt under the foot.

ANN.

Why Phyllis can't be satisfied with a cook-general passes my comprehension ——

ROSE.

[*Wearily.*] Oh, shut up !

JAMES.

Steady, mother!

THADDEUS.

[*Looking at them all.*] Ah, you've never liked Phyllis from the beginning, any of you.

LOUISA.

Never liked her!

THADDEUS.

Never cottoned to her, never appreciated her. Oh, I know—old Mr. Burdock's shop! [*Simply.*] Well, Ann; well, Lou; shop or no shop, there's no better wife—no better woman—breathing than Phyl.

LOUISA.

One may like a person without being blind to short-comings.

ANN.

Nobody's flawless—nobody.

LOUISA.

There are two sides to every person as well as to every question, I always maintain.

THADDEUS.

However, maybe it won't matter so much in the future. It hasn't made things easier for us in the past. [*Snapping his fingers softly.*] But now ——

STEPHEN.

[*Caustically.*] Henceforth you and your wife will be above the critical opinion of others, eh, Tad?

JAMES.

Aye, Tad's come into money now.   Mind what you're at, mother!   Be careful, Lou!   Tad's come into money.

THADDEUS.

[*In a quiet voice, but clenching his hands tightly.*] My God, I hope I have!   I'm not a hypocrite, Jim.   My God, I hope I have!
[*The door opens and* ELKIN *appears.*

ELKIN.

Miss Thornhill is here.  [*There is a general movement.* THADDEUS *walks away to the fireplace.* JAMES, STE-PHEN, *and* PONTING *also rise and* ROSE *joins* PONTING *at the library-table.*   ANN *and* LOUISA *shake out their skirts formidably, their husbands taking up a position near them.* HELEN THORNHILL *enters, followed by* VALLANCE, *who closes the door.* ELKIN *presents* HELEN.] Miss Thornhill. [*To* HELEN, *pointing to the group on the left.*]  These gentlemen are the late Mr. Mortimore's brothers.  [*Pointing to* ROSE.]  His sister.

HELEN.

[*A graceful, brilliant-looking girl with perfectly refined manners, wearing an elegant traveling-dress—almost inaudibly.*] Oh, yes.

ELKIN.

[*With a wave of the hand towards the others.*]  Members of the family by marriage.
[*She sits, at* ELKIN'S *invitation, in the chair beside the writing-table.   The attitude of the* JAMES *and* STEPHEN MORTIMORES, *and of the* PONTINGS, *undergoes a marked change.*

JAMES.

[*After a pause, advancing a step or two.*]  I'm the eldest brother. [*Awkwardly.*]  James, I am.

STEPHEN.

[*Drawing attention to himself by an uneasy cough.*]
Stephen.

ANN.

[*Humbly.*] I'm Mrs. James.

LOUISA.

[*In the same tone.*] Mrs. Stephen.

ROSE.

[*Seating herself on the left of the library-table.*] Rose—
Mrs. Ponting. [*Glancing at* PONTING.] My husband.

THADDEUS.

[*Now standing behind the writing-table.*] Thaddeus.
My wife is up-stairs, trying on her ——
    [*He checks himself and retreats, again sitting at
    the centre window.*

JAMES.

[*Seating himself at the writing-table.*] Tired, I dessay?

HELEN.

[*Who has received the various announcements with a
dignified inclination of the head.*] A little.

STEPHEN.

[*Bringing forward the armchair from the fireplace.*]
You weren't in Paris, Mr. Elkin tells us, when his
letter —— ?

HELEN.

No; I was nearly a nine hours' journey from Paris,
staying with friends at St. Etienne.

ROSE.

A pity.

LOUISA.

Great pity.                                    .

HELEN.

Mr. Elkin's letter was re-posted and reached me on Wednesday. I got back to Paris that night.

ELKIN.

[*Seating himself beside her.*] And had a hard day's traveling again yesterday.

STEPHEN.

[*Sitting in the armchair.*] She must be worn out.

ANN.

Indeed she must.

PONTING.

[*Sitting by* ROSE.] Hot weather, too. Most exhausting.

ELKIN.

[*To* HELEN.] And you were out and about this morning with Mrs. Elkin before eight, I heard?

HELEN.

She brought me round here.

ELKIN.

[*Sympathetically.*] Ah, yes.

JAMES.

Round here? [ELKIN *motions significantly towards the ceiling.*] Oh—aye. [*After another pause, to* HELEN.] When did you see him last—alive?

##### Helen.

In April. He spent Easter with me. [*Unobtrusively opening a little bag which she carries and taking out a handkerchief.*] We always spent our holidays together. [*Drying her eyes.*] I was to have met him at Rouen on the fifteenth of next month ; we were going to Etretat.

##### Elkin.

[*After a further silence.*] Er—h'm!—the principal business we are here to discuss is, I presume, the question of Miss Thornhill's future.

##### Helen.

[*Quickly.*] Oh, no, please.

##### Elkin.

No?

##### Helen.

If you don't mind, I would rather my future were taken for granted, Mr. Elkin, without any discussion.

##### Elkin.

Taken for granted ?

##### Helen.

I am no worse off than thousands of other young women who are suddenly thrown upon their own resources. I'm a great deal better off than many, for there's a calling already open to me—art. My prospects don't daunt me in the least.

##### Elkin.

No, no; nobody wants to discourage you——

##### Helen.

[*Interrupting* Elkin.] I confess—I confess I am disappointed—hurt—that father hasn't made even a slight

provision for me—not for the money's sake, but because
—because I meant so much to him, I've always believed.
He *would* have made me secure if he had lived longer, I
am convinced.

ELKIN.

[*Soothingly.*]  Not improbable ; not improbable.

HELEN.

But I don't intend to let my mind dwell on that.  What
I do intend to think is that, in leaving me with merely
my education and the capacity for earning my living, he
has done more for my happiness—my real happiness—
than if he had left me every penny he possessed.  With
no incentive to work, I might have drifted by and by into
an idle, aimless life.  I *should* have done so.

STEPHEN.

A very rational view to take of it.

PONTING.

Admirable !
        [ *There is a nodding of heads and a murmur of ap-
        proval from the ladies.*

ELKIN.

Very admirable and praiseworthy.  [*To the others,
diplomatically.*]  But we are not to conclude that Miss
Thornhill declines to entertain the idea of some—some
arrangement which would enable her to embark upon her
artistic career ——

HELEN.

Yes, you are.  I don't need assistance, and I couldn't
accept it.  [*Flaring up.*]  I will accept nothing that
hasn't come to me direct from my father—nothing.

[*Softening.*] But I am none the less grateful to you, dear Mr. Elkin—[*looking round*] to everybody—for this kindness.

STEPHEN.

[*With a sigh.*] So be it ; so be it, if it must be so.

PONTING.

We don't wish to *force* assistance upon Miss Thornhill.

STEPHEN.

On the contrary ; we respect her independence of character.
[ELKIN *shrugs his shoulders at* VALLANCE, *who is now seated upon the settee on the right.*

JAMES.

[*Stroking his beard.*] Art—art. You've been studying painting, haven't you?

HELEN.

At Julian's, in the Rue de Berri, for three years—for pleasure, I imagined.

JAMES.

[*Glancing furtively at* ANN.] D'ye do oil portraits—family groups and so on?

HELEN.

I'm not very successful as a colorist. Black and white is what I am best at.

JAMES.

[*Dubiously.*] Black and white ——

STEPHEN.

Is there much demand for that form of art in Paris?

HELEN.

Paris? Oh, I shall come to London.

JAMES.

London, eh?

HELEN.

My drawing isn't quite good enough for over there. It's only good enough for England. I shall sell my jewellery and furniture—I'm sharing a flat in the Avenue de Messine with an American girl—and that will carry me along excellently till I'm fairly started. Oh, I shall do very well.

ROSE.

I live in London. My house will be somewhere for you to drop into, whenever you feel inclined.

HELEN.

Thank you.

PONTING.

[*Pulling at his moustache.*] Often as you like—often as you like ——

ROSE.

[*Loftily.*] As I am in "society," as they call it, that will be nice for you.

JAMES.

[*To* ANN.] Now, then, mother, don't you be behindhand ——

ANN.

I'm sure I shall be very pleased if Miss Thornton ——

A MURMUR.

Thornhill ——

ANN.

If she'll pay us a visit. We're homely people, but she and Cissy could play tennis all day long.

LOUISA.

If she does come to Singlehampton, she mustn't go away without staying a day or two in the Crescent. [*To* HELEN.] Do you play chess, dear? [HELEN *shakes her head.*] My husband will teach you—won't you, Stephen?

STEPHEN.

Honored.

THADDEUS.

[*Who has risen and come forward.*] I'm sorry my wife isn't here. We should be grieved if Miss Thornhill left us out in the cold.

HELEN.

[*Looking at him with interest.*] You are father's musical brother, aren't you?

THADDEUS.

Yes—Tad.

HELEN.

[*With a faint smile.*] I promise not to leave you out in the cold. [*To everybody.*] I can only repeat, I am most grateful. [*To* ELKIN, *about to rise.*] Mrs. Elkin is waiting for me, to take me to the dressmaker——

ELKIN.

[*Detaining her.*] One moment—one moment. [*To the others.*] Gentlemen, Mr. Vallance and I have had our little talk and we agree that the proper course to pursue in the matter of the late Mr. Mortimore's estate is to proceed at once to insert an advertisement in the public journals.

JAMES.

An advertisement?

ELKIN.

With the object of obtaining information respecting any
will which he may have made at any time.

JAMES.

[*After a pause.*] Oh—very good.

STEPHEN.

[*Coldly.*] Does Mr. Vallance really advise that this is
the proper course?

[VALLANCE *rises and* THADDEUS *again retires.*

VALLANCE.

[*Assentingly.*] In the peculiar circumstances of the
case.

ELKIN.

We propose also to go a step further.   We propose to
circularize.

JAMES.

Circularize?

PONTING.

[*Disturbed.*] What the dev—what's that?

ELKIN.

We propose to address a circular to every solicitor in
the law-list asking for such information.

HELEN.

[*To* ELKIN.] Is this necessary?

ELKIN.

Mr. Vallance will tell us ——

VALLANCE.

It comes under the head of taking all reasonable measures to find a will.

HELEN.

[*Looking round.*] I—I sincerely hope that no one will
think that it is on my behalf that Mr. Elkin ——

ELKIN.

[*Checking her.*] My dear, these are formal, and ami-
cable, proceedings, to which *everybody*, we suggest,
should be a party.

VALLANCE.

Everybody.

ELKIN.

[*Invitingly.*] Everybody.

JAMES.

[*Breaking a chilly silence.*] All right.   Go ahead, Mr.
Elkin. [*To* STEPHEN.] We're willing?

STEPHEN.

Why not ; why not? Rose ——?

ROSE.

[*Hastily.*] Oh, certainly.

VALLANCE.

[*To* JAMES.] I have your authority, Mr. Mortimore,
for acting with Mr. Elkin in this matter?

JAMES.

You have, sir.

ELKIN.

[*To* VALLANCE, *rising.*] Will you come round to my
office with me?
> [HELEN *rises with* ELKIN, *whereupon the other*
> *men get to their feet.* ANN *and* LOUISA *also*
> *rise as* HELEN *comes to them and offers her*
> *hand.*

ANN.

[*Shaking hands.*] We're at the Grand Hotel——

LOUISA.

[*Shaking hands.*] So am I and my husband.

HELEN.

I'll call, if I may.
> [*She shakes hands with* STEPHEN *and* JAMES *and*
> *goes to* ROSE.

ROSE.

[*Rising to shake hands with her.*] We're at the Grand
too.  Colonel Ponting and I would be delighted ——

PONTING.

Delighted.
> [HELEN *merely bows to* PONTING ; *then she shakes*
> *hands with* THADDEUS *and passes out into the*
> *hall.*

ELKIN.

[*Who has opened the door for* HELEN—*to everybody,*
*genially.*] Good-day ; good-day.

JAMES *and* STEPHEN.

Good-day, Mr. Elkin.   Good-day.
> [ELKIN *follows* HELEN.

VALLANCE.

[*At the door—to* JAMES *and* STEPHEN.] Where can I
see you later?

JAMES.

The Grand. Food at half-past one.

VALLANCE.

Thank you very much.
[*He bows to the ladies and withdraws, closing the
door after him.*

PONTING.

[*Pacing the room indignantly.*] I wouldn't give the
fellow so much as a dry biscuit!
[*There is a general break up,* ANN *and* LOUISA
*joining* ROSE *on the right.*

JAMES.

[*Pacifically.*] Oh, there's no occasion to upset yourself, Colonel.

PONTING.

[*On the left.*] I wouldn't! I wouldn't! He's against
us on every point.

JAMES.

Let 'em advertise, if it amuses 'em. [*In an outburst.*]
Let 'em advertise *and* circularize till they're blue in the
face.

ROSE.

[*With a shrill laugh.*] Jim! Ha! ha! ha!

ANN *and* LOUISA.

[*Solemnly.*] Hus—s—sh!

JAMES.

[*Dropping to a whisper.*] Oh, I—I forgot.

STEPHEN.

Yes, yes, yes; it's nothing more than a lawyer's trick, to swell their bill of costs.

JAMES.

Of course it isn't; of course it isn't. [*Passing his hand under his beard.*] I want some air, mother. Get out o' this.

ANN.

[*Fastening her mantle.*] You've an appointment at the tailor's, remember.

STEPHEN.

[*Looking at his watch.*] So have I.

JAMES.

Are you coming, Colonel? [*Finding himself in the centre of a group—with a change of manner.*] I say: What a beautiful girl, this girl of Ned's!

STEPHEN.

Exceedingly.

PONTING.

[*Producing his cigarette-case.*] Charming young woman.

ANN *and* LOUISA.

Lovely.   A lovely girl.

ROSE.

Quite presentable.

JAMES.

And she doesn't ask a shilling of us—not a bob.

STEPHEN.

She impressed me enormously.

PONTING.

[*An unlighted cigarette in his mouth.*] Charming ; charming.

JAMES.

Ned ought to have left her a bit ; he ought to have left her a bit. [*Resolutely.*] Mother—we'll have her down home.

STEPHEN.

We must tell some fib or other as to who she is. Yes, we'll show her a little hospitality.

PONTING.

And Rose—in London. That'll make it up to her.

ROSE.

Yes, that'll make it up to her.
[*The ladies move into the hall; the men follow.*

JAMES.

[*In the doorway—to* THADDEUS, *who is now seated at the writing-table.*] Tad, I'll stand you and your wife a good lunch. One-thirty.
[THADDEUS *nods acceptance and* JAMES *goes after the others.* THADDEUS *rises, and, looking through the blind of the middle window, watches them depart. Presently* PHYLLIS *appears, putting on her gloves.*

PHYLLIS.

[*At the door, drawing a breath of relief.*] They've gone.

THADDEUS.

[*Turning.*] Is that you, Phyl?

PHYLLIS.

[*Coming further into the room.*] I've been waiting on
the landing.

THADDEUS.

Why didn't you come back, dear? You've missed
Miss Thornhill.

PHYLLIS.

[*Walking away to the left, working at the fingers of a
glove.*] Yes, I—I know.

THADDEUS.

The very person we were all here to meet.

PHYLLIS.

I—I came over nervous. [*Eagerly.*] What is she like?

THADDEUS.

Such an aristocratic-looking girl.

PHYLLIS.

Is she—is she ?

THADDEUS.

I'll tell you all about her by and by. [*Pushing the door
to and coming to* PHYLLIS, *anxiously.*] What do you think
they're going to do now, Phyl?

PHYLLIS.

Who?

THADDEUS.

The lawyers.  They're going to advertise.

PHYLLIS.

Advertise ?

THADDEUS.

In the papers—to try to discover a will.

PHYLLIS.

I—I suppose that's a mere matter of form ?

THADDEUS.

Elkin and Vallance say so. According to Stephen, it's simply a lawyer's dodge to run up costs. [*Brightening.*] Anyhow, we mustn't complain, where a big estate is involved ——

PHYLLIS.

Is it—such a—big estate ?

THADDEUS.

Guess.

PHYLLIS.

I can't.

THADDEUS.

[*Coming closer to her.*] I heard Elkin's managing-clerk tell Jim and the Colonel this morning that poor Ned may have died worth anything between a hundred and fifty and two hundred thousand pounds.

PHYLLIS.

[*Faintly.*] Two hundred thousand ——!

THADDEUS.

Yes.

PHYLLIS.

Oh, Tad ——!
> [*She sits, on the settee on the left, leaning her head upon her hands.*

THADDEUS.

Splitting the difference, and allowing for death duties, our share would be close upon forty thousand. To be on the safe side, put it at thirty-nine thousand. Thirty-nine thousand pounds! [*Moving about the room excitedly.*] I've been reckoning. Invest that at four per cent.—one is justified in calculating upon a four per cent. basis—invest thirty-nine thousand at four per cent., and there you have an income of over fifteen hundred a year. Fifteen hundred a year! [*Returning to her.*] When we die, seven hundred and fifty a year for Joyce, seven hundred and fifty for Cyril! [*She rises quickly and clings to him, burying her head upon his shoulder and clutching at the lapel of his coat.*] Poor old lady! [*Putting his arms round her.*] Poor old lady! You've gone through such a lot, haven't you?

PHYLLIS.

[*Sobbing.*] We both have.

THADDEUS.

Sixteen years of it.

PHYLLIS.

Sixteen years.

THADDEUS.

Of struggle—struggle and failure.

PHYLLIS.

Failure brought upon you by your wife—by me.

THADDEUS.

Nonsense—nonsense ——

PHYLLIS.

You always call it nonsense ; you know it's true.   If you hadn't married me—if you'd married a girl of better family—you wouldn't have lost caste in the town ——

THADDEUS.

Hush, hush !   Don't cry, Phyl ; don't cry, old lady.

PHYLLIS.

You'd have had the choral societies, and the High School, and the organ at All Saints ;  you'd have been at the top of the tree long ago.   You know you would !

THADDEUS.

[*Rallying her.*] And if *you* hadn't married *me*, you might have captivated a gay young officer at Claybrook and got to London eventually.   Rose did it, and you might have done it.   So that makes us quits.   Don't cry.

PHYLLIS.

[*Gradually regaining her composure.*] There *was* a young fellow at the barracks who was after me.

THADDEUS.

[*Nodding.*] You were prettier than Rose, a smarter girl altogether.

PHYLLIS.

[*Drying her eyes.*] I'll be smart again now, dear.   I'm only thirty-five.   What's thirty-five !

THADDEUS.

The children won't swallow up everything now, will they ?

PHYLLIS.

No; but Joyce shall look sweeter and daintier than ever, though.

THADDEUS.

Cyril shall have a first-class, public-school education ; that I'm determined upon.  There's Rugby—Rugby's the nearest—or Malvern ——

PHYLLIS.

[*With a catch in her breath.*]  Oh, but—Tad—we'll leave Singlehampton, won't we?

THADDEUS.

Permanently ?

PHYLLIS.

Yes—yes ——

THADDEUS.

Won't that be rather a mistake?

PHYLLIS.

A mistake !

THADDEUS.

Just as we're able to hold up our heads in the town.

PHYLLIS.

We should never be able to hold up our heads in Singlehampton.  If we were clothed in gold, we should still be lepers underneath ; the curse would still rest on us.

THADDEUS.

[*Bewildered.*]  But where—where shall we ——?

PHYLLIS.

I don't care—anywhere. [*Passionately.*] Anywhere
where I'm not sneered at for bringing up my children
decently, and for making my home more tasteful than
my neighbors'; anywhere where it isn't known that
I'm the daughter of a small shopkeeper—the daughter
of "old Burdock of West Street"! [*Imploringly.*] Oh,
Tad——!

THADDEUS.

You're right. Nothing is ever forgiven you in the
place you're born in. We'll clear out.

PHYLLIS.

[*Slipping her arm through his.*] When—when will you
get me away?

THADDEUS.

Directly, directly; as soon as the lawyers——
[*He pauses, looking at her blankly.*

PHYLLIS.

[*Frightened.*] What's the matter?

THADDEUS.

We—we're talking as if—as if Ned's money is already
ours!

PHYLLIS.

[*Withdrawing her arm—steadily.*] It will be.

THADDEUS.

Will it, do you think——?

PHYLLIS.

[*With an expressionless face.*] I prophesy—it will be.
[HEATH *enters and, seeing* THADDEUS *and*
PHYLLIS, *draws back.*

HEATH.

I'm sorry, sir.    I thought the room was empty.

THADDEUS.

We're going.  [*As he and* PHYLLIS *pass out into the hall.*]  Don't come to the door.

HEATH.

Thank you, sir.

    [HEATH *quietly and methodically replaces the chair at the window on the right.  Then, after a last look round, he switches off the lights and leaves the room again in gloom.*

**END OF THE FIRST ACT**

# THE SECOND ACT

*The scene represents the drawing-room of a modern, cheaply-built villa. In the wall at the back are two windows. One is a bay-window provided with a window-seat ; the other, the window on the right, opens to the ground into a small garden. At the bottom of the garden a paling runs from left to right, and in the paling there is a gate which gives access to a narrow lane. Beyond are the gardens and backs of other houses.*

*The fireplace is on the right of the room, the door on the left. A grand pianoforte, with its head towards the windows, and a music-stool occupy the middle of the room. On the right of the music-stool there is an arm-chair, and against the piano, facing the fireplace, there is a settee. Another settee faces the audience at the further end of the fireplace, and on the nearer side, opposite this settee, is an armchair. Also on the right hand, but nearer to the spectator, there is a round table. An ottoman, opposing the settee by the piano, stands close to the table.*

*At the end of the piano there is a small table with an arm-chair on its right and left, and on the extreme left of the room stands another armchair with a still smaller table beside it. On the left of the bay-window there is a writing-table, and in front of the writing-table, but turned to the window, a chair. Other articles of furniture fill spaces against the walls.*

*There is a mirror over the fireplace and a clock on the*

65

*mantel-shelf, and lying upon the round table are a hat
and a pair of gloves belonging to* HELEN. *Some flowers
in pots hide the empty grate.*
*The room and everything in the room are eloquent of nar-
row means, if not of actual poverty. But the way in
which the cheap furniture is dressed up, and the manner
of its arrangement about the room, give evidence of taste
and refinement.*
*The garden is full of the bright sunshine of a fine July
afternoon.*
THADDEUS *is at the piano accompanying a sentimental ballad
which* TRIST, *standing beside him, is singing.* PHYLLIS,
*looking more haggard than when last seen, is on the
settee by the fireplace. Her hands lie idly upon some
needlework in her lap and she is in deep thought.*
HELEN, *engaged in making a sketch of* JOYCE *and*
CYRIL, *who are facing her, is sitting in the chair on
the right of the table at the end of the piano. A
drawing-block is on her knees and a box of crayons on
the table at her elbow.* HELEN *and the* THADDEUS
MORTIMORES *are dressed in mourning, but not oppress-
ively so.*

### THADDEUS.

[*Taking his hands from the key-board—to* TRIST.] No,
no. Fill your lungs, man, fill your lungs.
          [PHYLLIS, *roused by the break in the music, picks
          up her work.*

### TRIST.

[*A big, healthy-looking, curly-headed young fellow in
somewhat shabby clerical clothes.*] I'm afraid it's no good,
my dear chap. The fact is, air will not keep in my
lungs.

.

THADDEUS.

[*Starting afresh with the symphony.*] Once more ——

HELEN.

[*To the children, softly.*] Do you want a rest?

CYRIL.

[*A handsome boy of fourteen, standing close to his sister.*] No, thanks.

JOYCE.

[*In the chair on the extreme left—a slim, serious child, a year older than* CYRIL.] Oh, no; don't give us a rest.
[*As the symphony ends, the door opens a little way and* JAMES *pops his head in.*

JAMES.

Hallo!

THADDEUS.

Hallo, Jim!
[JAMES *enters, followed by* STEPHEN ; *both with an air of bustle and self-importance. They also are in mourning, are gloved, and are wearing their hats which they remove on entering.*

STEPHEN.

May we come in?

JAMES.

Good-afternoon, Mr. Trist.

STEPHEN.

How do you do, Mr. Trist?

TRIST.

[*To* JAMES *and* STEPHEN.] How are you; how **are** you?

JAMES.

[*To the children, kissing* JOYCE.] Well, kids! [*Shaking hands with* HELEN.] Well, my dear! [*Crossing to* PHYLLIS, *who rises.*] Don't get up, Phyllis. What's this? You're not very bobbish, I hear.

PHYLLIS.

[*Nervously.*] It's nothing.

THADDEUS.

[*Tidying his music.*] She's sleeping badly just now, poor old lady.

STEPHEN.

[*Who has greeted* HELEN *and the children—to* PHYLLIS.] Oh, Phyllis, Louisa has discovered a wonderful cure for sleeplessness at the herbalist's in Crown Street. A few dried leaves merely. You strew them under the bed and the effect is magical.

JAMES.

Glass of warm milk's *my* remedy ——

STEPHEN.

Eighteen-pence an ounce, it costs.

JAMES.

Not that sleeplessness bothers *me*.

PHYLLIS.

[*Sitting on the ottoman and resuming her work—to* STEPHEN.] Thank you for telling me about it.

JAMES.

[*To* HELEN.] Making quite a long stay here.

HELEN.

[*Smiling.*] Am I not?

STEPHEN.

You and Phyllis, Tad, are more honored than we were in the Crescent.

JAMES.

Or we were at "Ivanhoe." She was only a couple o' nights with us.

STEPHEN.

*Less* with us. She arrived one morning and left the next.

JAMES.

[*To* HELEN.] Been in Nelson Villas over a week, haven't you?

HELEN.

[*Touching her drawing.*] Is it more than a week?

JAMES.

[*Looking at* HELEN'S *drawing.*] Taking the youngsters' portraits, too.

STEPHEN.

[*Also looking at the drawing.*] H'm! I suppose children *are* difficult subjects.

TRIST.

[*Moving towards the door—to* HELEN.] Miss Thornhill, don't forget your engagement.

HELEN.

[*To* JOYCE *ana* CYRIL.] Mr. Trist is going to treat us to the flower-show by and by.

CYRIL.

Good man!

JOYCE.

Oh, Mr. Trist!

STEPHEN.

[*To* TRIST.] Not driving you away, I hope?

TRIST.

[*At the door.*] No, no; I've some work to do.
[*He withdraws.* STEPHEN *puts his hat on the top
of the piano.*

JAMES.

[*After watching the door close.*] Decent sort o' young
man, that; nothing of the lodger about him.

STEPHEN.

I've always said so. [*To* THADDEUS, *lowering his
voice.*] Mr. Trist knows how—er—h'm—poor Edward
left his affairs?

THADDEUS.

Everybody does; it's all over the town.

STEPHEN.

[*Resignedly.*] Yes ; impossible to keep it to ourselves.

JAMES.

Thanks to their precious advertisement. [*To* JOYCE
*and* CYRIL, *loudly.*] Now, then, children; be off with
you! I want to talk to your father and mother.

JOYCE.

[*To* HELEN.] Will you excuse us?

CYRIL.

Awfully sorry, Helen.

[*The children pass through the open window into the garden and disappear.* HELEN *rises and, having laid her drawing-block aside, is following them.*

JAMES.

[*To* HELEN.] Not you, my dear. You're welcome to hear our business.

HELEN.

Oh, no; you mustn't let me intrude.

STEPHEN.

I think Helen *ought* to hear it. [HELEN *pauses, standing by the table on the right.*] I think she ought to be made aware of what's going on.

JAMES.

Tad ——

THADDEUS.

[*Coming forward.*] Eh?

JAMES.

The meeting's to take place this afternoon.
[PHYLLIS *looks up from her work suddenly, with parted lips.*

THADDEUS.

This afternoon?

STEPHEN.

At four o'clock.

THADDEUS.

[*Glancing at the clock on the mantelpiece.*] It's past three now.

##### JAMES.

[*Placing his hat on the table at the end of the piano and sitting at the left of the table.*] It's been fixed up at last rather in a hurry.

##### STEPHEN.

[*Sitting in the chair on the extreme left.*] We didn't get Elkin's letter, telling us he was coming through, till this morning.

##### THADDEUS.

You might have notified us earlier, though, one of you. Just like you fellows!

##### STEPHEN.

[*Waving his arms.*] On the day I go to press I've quite enough to remember.

##### JAMES.

[*To* THADDEUS, *roughly.*] It's your holiday-time ; what have *you* got to do? An hour's notice is as good as a week's.

##### STEPHEN.

[*To* HELEN.] This is a meeting of the family, Helen, to be held at my brother's house, for the purpose of— er ——

##### HELEN.

[*Advancing a little.*] Winding matters up?

##### JAMES.

For the purpose of receiving Elkin and Vallance's report.

##### HELEN.

[*Keenly.*] And to ——?

JAMES.

And to decide upon the administration of the estate on
behalf of the next-of-kin.

HELEN.

In my words—wind matters up. [*With an appearance
of cheerfulness.*] Which means an end to a month's suspense, doesn't it?

THADDEUS.

[*Apologetically.*] A not very satisfactory end to yours.

HELEN.

To mine? [*With an effort.*] Oh, I—I've suffered no
suspense, Mr. Tad. Mr. Elkin has kept me informed of
the result of the advertising and the circularizing from
the beginning.

THADDEUS.

But there has been no result.

HELEN.

No result *is* the result.

STEPHEN.

Exactly.
> [*During the following talk*, HELEN *moves away
> and seats herself in the chair by the head of the
> piano.* PHYLLIS *has resumed her work again,
> bending over it so that her face is almost hidden.*

THADDEUS.

[*To* JAMES *and* STEPHEN.] Will Rose and the Colonel
be down?

JAMES.

We're on our way to the station to meet 'em.

STEPHEN.

[*Bitterly.*] Ha! Will they be down?

THADDEUS.

You didn't overlook *them*, evidently.

JAMES.

[*With a growl.*] No; the gallant Colonel doesn't give
us much chance of overlooking *him*.

STEPHEN.

Colonel Ponting might be the only person interested,
judging by the tone he adopts.

JAMES.

A nice life he's been leading us lately.

STEPHEN.

Elkin and Vallance are sick of him.

JAMES.

Hasn't two penny pieces to clink together; that's the
size of it.

STEPHEN.

A man may be hard up and yet behave with dignity.

JAMES.

I expect the decorators are asking for a bit on the nail.

THADDEUS.

[*Sitting on the right of the table at the end of the piano.*]
Decorators?

STEPHEN.

[*To* THADDEUS.] Haven't you heard ——?

THADDEUS.

No.

STEPHEN.

The magnificent house they've taken in Carlos Place ——?

JAMES.

Close to Berkeley Square.

STEPHEN.

[*Correcting* JAMES'S *pronunciation.*] *Bark*eley Square.

JAMES.

Stables and motor-garridge at the back.

STEPHEN.

Oh, yes; they're decorating and furnishing most elaborately. Lou had a note from Rose a day or two since.

JAMES.

He'll strip my sister of every penny she's come into, if she doesn't look out.

STEPHEN.

The gross indelicacy of the thing is what offends me. *We* have been content to remain passive.

JAMES.

And I fancy our plans and projects are as important as the Colonel's.

STEPHEN.

I should assume so.

JAMES.

[*To* STEPHEN, *with a jerk of the thumb towards* THADDEUS.] Shall I ——?

STEPHEN.

No harm in it *now*.

JAMES.

[*To* THADDEUS, *leaning forward — impressively.*]
Tad ——

THADDEUS.

What?

JAMES.

That land at the bottom of Gordon Street, where the
allotment grounds are ——

THADDEUS.

Yes?

JAMES.

It's mine.

THADDEUS.

Yours, Jim?

JAMES.

It belongs to me.   I've signed the contract and paid a
deposit.

THADDEUS.

What do you intend to do with it?

JAMES.

What should I intend to do with it—eat it?   I intend
to build there—build the finest avenue of houses in
Singlehampton. [*Rising and going to the piano, where
he traces a plan on the lid with his finger.*] Look here!
[THADDEUS *joins him and watches the tracing of the
plan.*] Here's Gordon Street.   Here's the pub at the
corner.   I come alone here—straight along here—to
Albert Terrace.   Opposite Albert Terrace I take in
Clark's piano factory; and where Clark's factory stands

I lay out an ornamental garden with a fountain in the middle of it. On I go at a curve, to avoid the playground of Fothergill's school, till I reach Bolton's store. He stops me, but I'll squeeze him out some day, as sure as my name's James Henry! [*To* THADDEUS.] D'ye see?

THADDEUS.

[*Uncomfortably, eyeing* HELEN.] Splendid ; splendid.

JAMES.

[*Moving round the head of the piano to the right.*] Poor old Ned! Ha! my brother won't have done so badly by his native town after all.

THADDEUS.

[*Under his breath, trying to remind* JAMES *of* HELEN'S *presence.*] Jim—Jim ——

JAMES.

[*Obliviously, coming upon* HELEN.] D'ye know the spot we're talking about, my dear?

HELEN.

No.

JAMES.

You must get 'em to walk you down there. [*To* PHYLLIS.] You trot her down there, Phyllis.

PHYLLIS.

[*Without raising her eyes from her work.*] I will.

STEPHEN.

[*To* JAMES.] You haven't told them *everything*, Jim.

JAMES.

[*Sitting upon the settee by the piano.*] Haven't I ?
[*Mopping his brow.*] Oh, your offices ——

STEPHEN.

[*To everybody.*] It isn't of the greatest importance, perhaps, but it's part of James's scheme to erect an excep-
tionably noble building in the new road to provide ade-
quate printing and publishing offices for the *Times and
Mirror.*

THADDEUS.

What, you're not deserting King Street, Stephen ?

STEPHEN.

[*Rising and walking to the fireplace.*] Yes, I've had
enough of those cramped, poky premises.

THADDEUS.

They *are* inconvenient.

STEPHEN.

[*On the hearthrug, facing the others.*] And, to be perfectly frank, I've had enough of Mr. Hammond and the
*Courier.*

THADDEUS.

I don't blame you there. The *Courier* is atrociously
personal occasionally.

STEPHEN.

[*Pompously.*] I don't say it because Hammond is, in a
manner, my rival—I'm not so small-minded as that—but
I do say that he is a vulgar man and that the *Courier* is
a vulgar and mischievous journal.

JAMES.

He's up to date, though, is Mister Freddy Hammond.

STEPHEN.

His plant is slightly more modern than mine, I admit.

JAMES.

[*Chuckling.*] Aye, you'll be able to present those antediluvian printing-presses of yours to the museum as curiosities.

STEPHEN.

[*With a wave of the hand.*] Anyhow, the construction of Jim's new road marks a new era in the life of the *Times and Mirror.* [*Leaving the fireplace.*] I'm putting no less than twelve thousand pounds into the dear old paper, Tad.

THADDEUS.

[*Standing by the table on the left.*] Twelve thousand —— !

STEPHEN.

How will that agree with Mr. Hammond's digestion, eh? Twelve thousand pounds! [*Coming to* THADDEUS.] And what are *your* plans for the future, if one may ask? You'll leave these wretched villas, of course?

THADDEUS.

[*Evasively.*] Oh, I—I'm waiting till this law business is absolutely settled.

STEPHEN.

[*Hastily.*] Quite right; quite right. So am I; so am I, actually. But we may talk, I suppose, among ourselves ——

JAMES.

[*Looking at his watch and rising.*] By George! We shall miss Rose and the Colonel.

STEPHEN.

[*Fetching his hat.*]  Pish !  the Colonel.

JAMES.

[*Shaking hands hurriedly with* HELEN *who rises.*]
Ta-ta, my dear.  [*As he passes* PHYLLIS.]  See you at the
meeting, Phyllis.

STEPHEN.

[*To* HELEN, *across the piano.*]  Good-bye, Helen.

JAMES.

[*Who has picked up his hat, at the door.*]  Don't be late,
Tad.

STEPHEN.

[*At the door.*]  No, no ;  don't be late.

THADDEUS.

Four o'clock.

STEPHEN.

Sharp.
          [THADDEUS *follows* JAMES *and* STEPHEN *into the
          hall and returns immediately.*

THADDEUS.

[*Closing the door.*]  My dear Helen, I apologize to you
most humbly.

HELEN.

[*Coming forward.*]  For what?

THADDEUS.

For Jim's bad taste, and Stephen's, in talking before
you as they've been doing.

HELEN.

Oh, it's of no consequence.

THADDEUS.

I could have kicked Jim.

HELEN.

[*Impulsively.*] Mr. Tad—[*giving him her hand*] I congratulate you. [*Going to* PHYLLIS *and kissing her lightly upon the cheek.*] I congratulate you both heartily. No two people in the world deserve good fortune more than you do.

THADDEUS.

It's extremeiy kind and gracious of you to take it in this way.

HELEN.

Why, in what other way could I take it?

THADDEUS.

At your age, you mayn't esteem money very highly. But—there are other considerations——

HELEN.

[*Turning away and seating herself upon the settee by the piano.*] Yes, we won't speak of those.

THADDEUS.

[*Walking to the bay-window.*] And there was just a chance that the inquiries might have brought a will to light—a will benefiting you. Though you were anxious not to appear unfriendly to the family, you must have realized that.

HELEN.

Whether I did or not, it's all done with now finally— finally. [*Blowing the subject from her.*] Phew !

THADDEUS.

[*His elbows on the piano, speaking across it to* HELEN.]
Phyl and I are not altogether selfish and grasping.  She
has been worrying herself to death these last few days—
haven't you, Phyl?—ever since we heard the meeting
was near at hand.

PHYLLIS.

[*In a low voice.*]   Yes.

THADDEUS.

Ever since you came to us, in fact.

HELEN.

[*Jumping up.*]  Ah, what a nuisance I've been to you !
[*Sitting beside* PHYLLIS]   How relieved you'll be to pack
me off to-morrow !

THADDEUS.

To-morrow ?
[*Uttering a little sound,* PHYLLIS *stops working
and stares straight before her.*

HELEN.

[*Slipping an arm round* PHYLLIS'S *waist.*]  That letter
I had while we were at lunch—it was from a girl who
used to sit next to me at Julian's.  She's found me some
capital rooms, she says, close to Regent's Park, and I'm
going up to look at them.  [THADDEUS *comes to her.*]  In
any event, the sooner I get out of Singlehampton the
better.

THADDEUS.

Why ?

HELEN.

Everybody in the town eyes me so queerly ; I'm certain they suspect.

THADDEUS.

It's your imagination.

HELEN.

It isn't. [*Hesitatingly.*] I—I've confided in Mr. Trist.

THADDEUS.

[*Surprised.*] Confided in Trist?

HELEN.

[*Nodding.*] I hated the idea of his thinking me—deceitful.

THADDEUS.

[*Sitting on the settee by the piano.*] Trist would never have guessed.

HELEN.

Oh, Mr. Tad, who, in heaven's name, that wasn't born yesterday *could* believe the story of my being simply a *protégée* of father's, the daughter of an old business friend of his? Your brother Stephen may be an excellent editor, but his powers of invention are beneath contempt.

THADDEUS.

[*Laughing.*] Ha, ha, ha! [*Rubbing his knees.*] That's one for Stephen; that's a rap for Stephen.

HELEN.

And then, again, the other members of the family are becoming so horribly jealous.

THADDEUS.

[*Seriously.*] Ah, yes.

HELEN.

You noticed your brother's remarks? And Mrs.
James and Mrs. Stephen almost cut me in East Street
this morning.

THADDEUS.

[*Clenching his fists.*] Thank God, we shall have done
with that sort of thing directly we shake the dust of
Singlehampton from our feet!

HELEN.

Directly you——!

THADDEUS.

[*Gaily.*] There! Now I've let the cat out of the bag.
Phyllis will tell you. You tell her, Phyl. [*Rising.*] I
promised Rawlinson I'd help him index his madrigals
this afternoon; I'll run round to him and explain. [*Pausing on his way to the door.*] Helen, you must be our first
visitor in our new home, wherever we pitch our tent.
Make that a bargain with her, Phyl. [*At the door, to*
PHYLLIS.] We'll start at ten minutes to, old lady. Be
ready.

[*He disappears, closing the door after him.*

HELEN.

[*Rising and walking away to the left.*] Well! I do
think it shabby of you, Phyllis. You and Mr. Tad
might have trusted me with your secret. [*Facing her.*]
Phyllis, wouldn't it be glorious if you came to London to
live—or near London? Wouldn't it?

PHYLLIS.

[*In a strange, quiet voice, her hands lying quite still
upon her lap.*] Helen—Helen dear——

HELEN.

Yes?

PHYLLIS.

That morning, a month ago, in Linchpool—while we were all sitting in your poor father's library waiting for you ——

HELEN.

[*Returning to her.*] On the Friday morning ——

PHYLLIS.

There was a discussion as to making you an allowance, and—[*her eyes avoiding* HELEN'S] and everybody was most anxious—most anxious—that you should be placed upon a proper footing.

HELEN.

Mr. Elkin broached the subject when I arrived. You were out of the room.

PHYLLIS.

Yes. And you declined ——

HELEN.

Certainly. I gave them my reasons. Why do you bring this up?
>      [PHYLLIS *rises, laying her work upon the table
>      behind her.*

PHYLLIS.

[*Drawing a deep breath.*] Helen—I want you to reconsider your decision.

HELEN.

Reconsider it?

PHYLLIS.

I want you to reconsider your determination not to accept an allowance from the family.

HELEN.

Impossible.

PHYLLIS.

Oh, don't be so hasty.   Listen first.   This good fortune
of ours—of Tad's and mine—that you've congratulated
us upon—I shall never enjoy it ——

HELEN.

[*Incredulously.*]   Oh, Phyllis !

PHYLLIS.

I shall not.   It will never bring me a moment's happiness unless you consent to receive an allowance from the
family—[HELEN *seats herself in the chair on the extreme
left with her back to* PHYLLIS] sufficient to give you a
sense of independence ——

HELEN.

I couldn't.

PHYLLIS.

And to make your future perfectly safe.

HELEN.

I couldn't.

PHYLLIS.

[*Entreatingly.*]   Do—do ——

HELEN.

It's out of the question.

PHYLLIS.

Please—for my sake ——!

HELEN.

[*Turning to her.*] I'm sorry to distress you, Phyllis ; indeed I'm sorry. But when you see me gaining some little position in London, through my work, you'll cease to feel miserable about me.

PHYLLIS.

Never—never ——

HELEN.

[*Starting up and walking to the fireplace impetuously.*] Oh, you don't understand me—my pride. A pensioner of the Mortimore family ! I ! How can you suggest it ? I refused their help before I was fully acquainted with these, to me, uncongenial relations of father's—I don't include Mr. Tad in that expression, of course ; and now I *am* acquainted with them I would refuse it a thousand times. If I were starving, I wouldn't put myself under the smallest obligation to the Mortimores.

PHYLLIS.

[*Unsteadily.*] Obligation—to—the—Mortimores—obligation ——! [*As if about to make some communication to* HELEN, *supporting herself by leaning upon the table on the right, her body bent forward—almost inaudibly.*] Helen—Helen ——

HELEN.

What ——?

[*There is a short silence, and then* PHYLLIS *drops back upon the settee by the piano.*

PHYLLIS.

[*Rocking herself to and fro.*] Oh—oh, dear—oh ——!

HELEN.

[*Coming to her and standing over her.*] You're quite ill, Phyllis ; your bad nights are taking it out of you dreadfully. You ought to have the advice of a doctor.

PHYLLIS.

[*Weakly.*]  No—don't send for the doctor ——

HELEN.

Go up to your room, then, and keep quiet till Mr. Tad
calls you.  [*Glancing at the clock.*]  You've a quarter of
an hour ——

PHYLLIS.

[*Clutching* HELEN'S *skirt.*]  Helen—you're fond of me
and Tad—you said yesterday how attached you'd grown
to us ——

HELEN.

[*Soothingly.*]  I am—I am—very fond of you.

PHYLLIS.

And the children —— ?

HELEN.

Yes, yes.

PHYLLIS.

My poor children !

HELEN.

Hush !  Why *poor* children ?  Pull yourself together.
Go up to your room.

PHYLLIS.

[*Taking* HELEN'S *hand and caressing it.*]  Helen—if
you won't accept an allowance from the entire family,
accept it from Tad and me.

HELEN.

No, no, no.

PHYLLIS.

Four—three hundred a year.

HELEN.

No.

PHYLLIS.

Two hundred.

HELEN.

No.

PHYLLIS.

We could spare it.  We shouldn't miss it ; we should
never miss it.

HELEN.

Not a penny.

PHYLLIS.

[*Rising and gripping* HELEN'S *shoulders.*]  You shall
—you shall accept it, Helen.

HELEN.

Phyllis !  [*Releasing herself and drawing back.*]  Phyllis,
you're very odd to-day.  You've got this allowance idea
on the brain.  Look here ; don't let's mention the subject again, or I—I shall be offended.

PHYLLIS.

[*Dully, hanging her head.*]  All right.  Very well.

HELEN.

Forgive me.  It happens to be just the one point I'm
sensitive upon.  [*Listening, then going to the open window.*]
Here are the children.  Do go up-stairs.  [*Calling into
the garden.*]  Hallo !  [PHYLLIS *leaves the room as* CYRIL
*and* JOYCE *appear outside the window.  The boy is carrying a few freshly-cut roses.*]  Now, then, children !  Isn't
it time we routed Mr. Trist out of his study ?

CYRIL.

[*Entering and going towards the door.*] I'll stir the old chap up. [*Remembering the nosegay.*] Oh —— [*Presenting it to* HELEN, *who comes forward with* JOYCE.] Allow me ——

HELEN.

For me? How sweet of you! [*Placing the flowers against her belt and then at her breast.*] Where shall I wear them—here, or here?

CYRIL.

Anywhere you like. [*Awkwardly.*] We sha'n't see anything nicer at the flower-show, I'm certain.

HELEN.

No; they're beautiful.

CYRIL.

[*His eyes on the carpet.*] I don't mean the flowers—

HELEN.

[*Inclining her head.*] Thank you. [*To* CYRIL, *who again makes for the door.*] Don't disturb mother. [*Moving away to the fireplace where, at the mirror over the mantel-shelf, she fixes the roses in her belt.*] She has to go to Claybrook Road with your father in a little while and I want her to rest.

CYRIL.

[*Pausing.*] She *is* seedy, isn't she? [*Puckering his brows.*] Going to Uncle Jim's, are they?

HELEN.

Yes.

CYRIL.

That's to do with our money, I expect.

HELEN.

[*Busy at the mirror.*] With your money?

CYRIL.

Father's come into a heap of money, you know.

JOYCE.

[*Reproachfully.*] Cyril!

CYRIL.

[*Not heeding her.*] So have Uncle Jim and Uncle Stephen and Aunt Rose.

HELEN.

I'm delighted.

CYRIL.

[*To* JOYCE, *who is signing to him to desist.*] Oh, what's the use of our keeping it dark any longer?

JOYCE.

We promised mother ——

CYRIL.

Ages ago. But you heard what father said to Uncle Stephen—it's all over the town. Young Pither says there's something about it in the paper.

HELEN.

The paper?

CYRIL.

The *Courier*—that fellow Hammond's paper. Hammond was beastly sarcastic about it last week, Pither says. [*Going to the door.*] I don't read the *Courier* myself. [*At the door he beckons to* JOYCE. *She joins him and his voice drops to a whisper.*] Besides—[*glancing significantly at* HELEN, *whose back is turned to them*] it'll make it easier for *us*. [*Nudging her.*] Now's your chance; do it now. [*Aloud.*] Give me five minutes, you two. I can't be seen at the flower-show in these togs.

> [*He withdraws. Having assured herself that the door is closed,* JOYCE *advances to* HELEN.

JOYCE.

Helen——

HELEN.

Hallo!

JOYCE.

[*Gravely.*] Have you a minute to spare?

HELEN.
[*Coming to the round table.*] Yes, dear.

JOYCE.

Helen, it's quite true we've come into a great deal of money. Uncle Edward, who lived at Linchpool— oh, you knew him, didn't you?—he was a friend of yours——

HELEN.
[*Nodding.*] He was a friend of mine.

JOYCE.

Uncle Edward has left his fortune to the family— [*breaking off*] you've been told already! ——

HELEN.

Well—yes.

JOYCE.

We haven't received our share yet; but we *shall*, as soon as it's all divided up. [*Timidly.*] Helen—[HELEN *seats herself upon the ottoman in an attitude of attention*] I needn't tell you this will very much improve father and mother's position.

HELEN.

Naturally.

JOYCE.

And mine and Cyril's, too. I'm to finish abroad, I believe.

HELEN.

Lucky brat.

JOYCE.

But it's Cyril I want to talk to you about—my brother Cyril——

HELEN.

Cyril?

JOYCE.

Cyril is to be entered for one of the principal public schools.

HELEN.

Is he?

JOYCE.

One of those schools which stamp a boy a gentleman for the rest of his life.

HELEN.

He is a gentleman, as it is. I've a high opinion of Cyril.

JOYCE.

Oh, I *am* glad to hear you say so, because—because ——

HELEN.

Because what? [JOYCE *turns away in silence to the settee by the piano.*] What are you driving at, Joicey?

JOYCE.

[*Lounging on the settee uneasily and inelegantly.*] Of course, Cyril's only fourteen at present; there's no denying that.

HELEN.

I suppose there isn't.

JOYCE.

But in three years' time he'll be seventeen, and in another three he'll be twenty.

HELEN.

[*Puzzled.*] Well?

JOYCE.

And at twenty you're a man, aren't you?

HELEN.

A young man.

JOYCE.

[*Seating herself, her elbows on her knees, examining her fingers.*] And even then he'd be content to wait.

HELEN.

To wait? What for?

JOYCE.

[*In a low voice.*] Cyril wishes to marry you some day, Helen.

HELEN.

[*After a pause, gently.*] Does he?

JOYCE.

He consulted me about it soon after you came to us, and I advised him to be quite sure of himself before he spoke to you. And he *is*, quite sure of himself.

HELEN.

And he's asked you to speak *for* him?

JOYCE.

He prefers my doing it. [*Looking, under her lashes, at* HELEN.] Are you furious?

HELEN.

Not a scrap.

JOYCE.

[*Transferring herself from the settee to the floor at* HELEN'S *feet—embracing her.*] Oh, that's lovely of you! I was afraid you might be.

HELEN.

Furious?

JOYCE.

[*Gazing at her admiringly.*] At our aiming so high. I was afraid you might consider that marrying Cyril would be marrying beneath you.

HELEN.

[*Tenderly.*] The girl who marries Cyril will have to be a far grander person than I am, Joyce, to be marrying beneath her.

JOYCE.

Oh, Cyril's all right in himself, and so is father.
Father's very retiring, but he's as clever a musician as
any in the midlands.   And mother is all right in *herself*.
[*Backing away from* HELEN.] It's not mother's fault;
it's her misfortune ——

HELEN.

Her misfortune —— ?

JOYCE.

[*Bitterly.*] Oh, I'll be bound they mentioned it at
" Ivanhoe " or at the Crescent.

HELEN.

Mentioned —— ?

JOYCE.

[*Between her teeth.*] The shop—grandfather's shop ——

HELEN.

Ah, yes.

JOYCE.

[*Clenching her hands.*]  Ah!  [*Squatting upon her heels,
her shoulders hunched.*]  Grandfather was a grocer, Helen
—a grocer.   Oh, mother has suffered terribly through it
—agonies.

HELEN.

Poor mother !

JOYCE.

We've all suffered.   Sometimes it's been as much as
Cyril and I could do to keep our heads up ; [*proudly,
with flashing eyes*] but we've done it.   The Singlehampton people are beasts.

HELEN.

Joyce!

JOYCE.

If it's the last word I ever utter—beasts. [*Swallowing a tear.*] And only half of it was grocery—only half.

HELEN.

Only half —— ?

JOYCE.

It was a double shop. There were two windows ; the other half was bottles of wine. They forget that ; they forget that!

HELEN.

A shame.

JOYCE.

[*Embracing* HELEN *again.*] What shall I say to him, then ?

HELEN.

Say to him ?

JOYCE.

Cyril—what answer shall I give him?

HELEN.

Oh, tell Cyril that I am highly complimented by his offer ——

JOYCE.

[*Eagerly.*] Complimented—yes —— ?

HELEN.

And that, if he's of the same mind when he's a man, and I am still single, he may propose to me again.

JOYCE.

[*In alarm.*]  If you're—still single ——?

HELEN.

Yes—[*shaking her head*] and if he's of the same mind.
   [*There is a sharp, prolonged rapping on the door.*
   JOYCE *and* HELEN *rise.*

JOYCE.

[*Going to the door.*]  It's that frightful tease.
   [*She opens the door and* TRIST *enters, carrying his*
   *hat, gloves, and walking-stick.*

TRIST.

Ladies, I have reason to believe that several choice
specimens of the *Dianthus Caryophyllus* refuse to raise
their heads until you grace the flower-show with your
presence.
   [JOYCE *slaps his hand playfully and disappears.*
   HELEN *takes her hat from the round table and,*
   *standing before the mirror at the mantelpiece,*
   *pins it on her head.*  TRIST *watches her.*

HELEN.

[*After a silence, her back to* TRIST.]  The glass reflects
more than one face, Mr. Trist.

TRIST.

[*Moving.*]  I beg your pardon.

HELEN.

You were thinking ——?

TRIST.

Philosophizing—observing your way of putting on your
hat.

HELEN.

I put it on carelessly?

TRIST.

Quickly.  A convincing sign of youth.  After you are five-and-twenty the process will take at least ten minutes.

HELEN.

And at thirty?

TRIST.

Half an hour.  Add another half-hour for each succeeding decade ——

HELEN.

[*Turning to him.*]  I'm afraid you're a knowing, worldly parson.

TRIST.

[*Laughing.*]  No, no; a tolerant, human parson.

HELEN.

We shall see.  [*Picking up her gloves.*]  If ever you get a living in London, Mr. Trist, I shall make a point of sitting under you.

TRIST.

I bind you to that.

HELEN.

[*Pulling on a glove.*]  By-the-bye, I set out to seek *my* London living to-morrow.

TRIST.

[*With a change of manner.*]  To-morrow?

HELEN.

To-morrow.

TRIST.

[*Blankly.*]  I—I'm sorry.

HELEN.

Very polite of you.   I'm glad.

TRIST.

Glad?

HELEN.

It sounds rather unkind, doesn't it?   Oh, I'm extremely fond of everybody in this house—Mr. and Mrs. Tad and the children, I mean.   But I'm sure it isn't good, morally, for me to be here, even if there were no other reasons for my departure.

TRIST.

Morally?

HELEN.

Yes ; if I remained here, all that's bad in my nature would come out on top.   Do you know that I've the makings in me of a most accomplished liar and hypocrite?

TRIST.

I shouldn't have suspected it.

HELEN.

I have.  [*Coming nearer to him.*]  What do you think takes place this afternoon?

TRIST.

What?

HELEN.

[*With gradually increasing excitement.*]  There's to be a meeting of the Mortimore family at James Mortimore's house at four o'clock. He and his brother Stephen have just informed me, with the delicacy which is characteristic of them, that they are going to arrange with the lawyers to administer my father's estate without any more delay. And I was double-faced enough to receive the news smilingly and agreeably, and all the time I could have struck them—I could have seen them drop dead in this room without a pang of regret ——

TRIST.

No, no ——

HELEN.

I could. [*Walking away and pacing the room on the left.*] Oh, it isn't father's money I covet. I said so to the family in Linchpool and I say it again. But I deceived myself.

TRIST.

Deceived yourself?

HELEN.

Deceived myself. I can't *bear* that father should have forgotten me. I can't bear it; I can't resign myself to it; I shall never resign myself to it. I thought I should be able to, but I was mistaken. I told Mr. Thaddeus that I've been suffering no suspense this last month. It's a falsehood; I've been suffering intense suspense. I've been watching the posts, for letters from Elkin; I've been praying, daily, hourly, that something—anything—might be found to prove that father had remembered me. And I loathe these people, who step over me and stand between me and the being I loved best on earth; I loathe them. I detest the whole posse of them, except the Thaddeuses; and I wish this money may bring them, and those belonging to them, every ill that's conceivable. [*Confronting* TRIST, *her bosom heaving.*] Don't you lecture me.

TRIST.

[*Good-humoredly.*] I haven't the faintest intention of doing so.

HELEN.

Ha! [*At the piano, mimicking* JAMES.] Here's Gordon Street——

TRIST.

Eh?

HELEN.

You come along here, to Albert Terrace—taking in Clark's piano factory ——

TRIST.

Who does?

HELEN.

[*Fiercely.*] Here—here's the pub at the corner!

TRIST.

[*Bewildered.*] I—I don't ——-

HELEN.

[*Speaking to him across the piano.*] James Mortimore is buying land and building a new street in the town.

TRIST.

Really?

HELEN.

And Stephen is putting twelve thousand pounds into his old-fashioned paper, to freshen it up ; and the Pontings are moving into a big house in London—near Burkeley Square, as James calls it ; and they must needs discuss their affairs in my hearing, brutes that they are!

[*Coming to the chair on the left of the table at the end of the piano.*] Oh, thank God, I'm leaving the town to-morrow! It was only a sort of curiosity that brought me here. [*Sitting and producing her handkerchief.*] Thank God, I'm leaving to-morrow!

> [*He walks to the window on the right to allow her to recover herself, and then returns to her.*

TRIST.

My dear child, may I speak quite plainly to you?

HELEN.

[*Wiping her eyes.*] If you don't lecture me.

TRIST.

I won't lecture you. I merely venture to suggest that you are a trifle illogical.

HELEN.

I dare say.

TRIST.

After all, recollect, our friends James and Stephen are not to be blamed for the position they find themselves in.

HELEN.

Their manners are insufferable.

TRIST.

Hardly insufferable. Nothing is insufferable.

HELEN.

There you go!

TRIST.

Their faults of manner and breeding are precisely the faults a reasonable, dispassionate person would have no difficulty in excusing.  And I shall be mucn astonished, when the bitterness of your mortification has worn off ——

HELEN.

You *are* lecturing !

TRIST.

I'm not ; I give you my word I'm not.

HELEN.

It sounds uncommonly like it.  What did I tell you the other day—that you were different from the clergy-men I'd met hitherto, because you were ——?

TRIST.

Jolly.

HELEN.

[*With a shrug.*]  Jolly !  [*Wearily.*]  Oh, please go and hurry the children up, and let's be off to the flowers.

TRIST.

[*Not stirring.*]  My dear Miss Thornhill ——

HELEN.

[*Impatiently.*]  I'll fetch them ——

TRIST.

Don't.  [*Deliberately.*]  My dear Miss Thornhill, to show you how little I regard myself as worthy of the privilege of lecturing you ;  [*smiling*] to show you how the seeds of selfishness may germinate and flourish even in the breast of a cleric—may I make a confession to you?

HELEN.

Confession —— ?

TRIST.

I—I want to confess to you that the circumstance of your having been left as you are—cast adrift on the world, unprotected, without means apart from your own talent and exertions—is one that fills me with—hope.

HELEN.

Hope ?

TRIST.

Fills me with hope, though it may scarcely justify my presumption. [*Sitting opposite to her.*] You were assuming a minute ago, in joke perhaps, the possibility of my obtaining a living some day.

HELEN.

[*Graciously, but with growing uneasiness.*] Not altogether in joke.

TRIST.

Anyhow, there *is* a decided possibility of a living coming my way—and practically in London, as it chances.

HELEN.

I—I'm pleased.

TRIST.

Yes, in the natural order of events a living will be vacant within the next few years which is in the gift of the father of an old college chum of mine. It's a suburban parish—close to Twickenham—and I'm promised it.

HELEN.

That would be—nice for you.

TRIST.

[*Gazing at her fixedly.*] Jolly.

HELEN.

[*Her eyes drooping.*] Very—jolly.

TRIST.

I should still be a poor man—that I shall always be ;
but poverty is relative.  It would be riches compared
with my curacy here.  [*After a pause.*] The vicarage
has a garden with some grand old trees.

HELEN.

Many of the old gardens—in the suburbs—are charming.

TRIST.

I—I could let the vicarage during the summer, to
increase my income.

HELEN.

May a vicar—let—his vicarage ?

TRIST.

It's done.  Some Bishops object to it ; [*innocently*] but
you can dodge the old boy.

HELEN.

Dodge the—old boy !

TRIST.

There are all sorts of legal fictions to help you.  I
know of a Bishop's son-in-law who let his vicarage for a
term under the pretence of letting only the furniture.

HELEN.

Wicked.

TRIST.

[*Leaning forward.*] But I shouldn't dream of letting
my vicarage if my income—proved sufficient ——

HELEN.

It would be wealth—you say—in comparison ——

TRIST.

Yes, but I—I might—marry.

HELEN.

[*Hastily.*] Oh—oh, of course.

[*The door opens and* JOYCE *and* CYRIL *enter, dressed for going out.* CYRIL *is in his best suit, is gloved, and swings a cane which is too long for him. At the same moment* THADDEUS *lets himself into the garden at the gate. He is accompanied by* DENYER, *an ordinary-looking person with whiskers and moustache.* HELEN *and* TRIST *rise, and she goes to the mirror in some confusion and gives a last touch to her hat.*

JOYCE.

Have we kept you waiting?

CYRIL.

Sorry. Couldn't get my tie to go right.

THADDEUS.

[*In the garden.*] Come in, Denyer. [*At the window, to those in the room.*] What, haven't you folks gone yet?

TRIST.

[*With the children, following* HELEN *into the garden.*] Just off.

THADDEUS.

[*To* HELEN, *as she passes him.*] Hope you'll enjoy yourself.

TRIST.

[*To* DENYER.] Ah, Mr. Denyer, how are you?

DENYER.

How are you, Mr. Trist?

JOYCE *and* CYRIL.

[*To* THADDEUS.] Good-bye, father.

THADDEUS.

[*Kissing them.*] Good-bye, my dears.
        [TRIST *opens the gate and* HELEN *and the children
        pass out into the lane.* TRIST *follows them,
        closing the gate.* THADDEUS *and* DENYER *en-
        ter the room.* DENYER *is carrying a news-
        paper.*

CYRIL.

[*Out of sight, shrilly.*] Which way?

TRIST.

Through Parker Street.

JOYCE.

Who walks with who?

HELEN.

I walk with Cyril.
        [*The sound of the chatter dies in the distance.*

DENYER.

[*To* THADDEUS.] Then I can put up the bill at once,
Mr. Mortimore?

THADDEUS.

[*Laying his hat upon the table on the left.*] Do, Denyer. To-morrow—to-day ——

DENYER.

I'll send a man round in the morning. [*Producing a
note-book and writing in it.*] Let's see—your lease is
seven, fourteen, twenty-one?

THADDEUS.

That's it.

DENYER.

How much of the first seven is there to run—I ought
to remember —— ?

THADDEUS.

Two years and a half from Michaelmas.

DENYER.

Rent?

THADDEUS.

Forty.
[*The door opens a little way and* PHYLLIS *peeps in.
Her features are drawn, her lips white and set.*

DENYER.

Fixtures at a valuation, I s'pose ?

THADDEUS.

Ha, ha !   The costly fixtures at a valuation.

DENYER.

You may as well sell 'em, if they only fetch tuppence.
[*Seeing* PHYLLIS, *who has entered softly.*]   Good-afternoon,
ma'am.

PHYLLIS.

[*In a low voice.*]   Good-afternoon.

THADDEUS.

[*Turning to her.*]   Phyl, dear!   I met Mr. Denyer in
the lane.   [*Gleefully.*]   The bill goes up to-morrow—

" house to let "—to-morrow morning—[*to* DENYER] first
thing ——

> [PHYLLIS *moves to the bay-window without
> speaking.*

DENYER.

First thing. [*Putting his pocketbook away.*] Excuse
me—you're on the lookout for a new residence ?

THADDEUS.

Oh—er—one must live somewhere, Denyer.

DENYER.

And a much superior house to *this*, Mr. Mortimore, I
lay a guinea.

THADDEUS.

[*Walking about with his hands in his pockets.*] The
children are springing up—getting to be tremendous
people.

DENYER.

[*Genially.*] Oh, come, sir! *We* know.

THADDEUS.

[*Pausing in his walk.*] Eh ?

DENYER.

Everybody in the town knows of your luck, and the
family's. [*Picking up his hat and newspaper, which he
has laid upon the ottoman.*] Here's another allusion to it
in this week's *Courier.*

THADDEUS.

The *Courier?*

DENYER.

[*Handing him the paper.*] Just out. You keep it; I've got another at 'ome. [THADDEUS *is searching the paper.*] Middle page—"Town Topics."

THADDEUS.

Thanks.

DENYER.

Mr. Hammond—he will poke his fun. [*Going to the window.*] P'r'aps you'll give us a call, sir?

THADDEUS.

[*Following him absently, reading.*] Yes, I'll call in.

DENYER.

[*To* PHYLLIS, *who is sitting in the chair by the bay-window.*] Good-day, ma'am. [*In the garden, to* THADDEUS, *persuasively.*] Now, you won't forget Gibson and Denyer, Mr. Mortimore?

THADDEUS.

[*At the window.*] I won't; I won't.

DENYER.

The old firm. [*Opening the gate.*] What we haven't got on our books isn't worth considering, you take it from me.

[*He disappears, closing the gate.* THADDEUS *comes back into the room.*

THADDEUS.

Upon my soul, this is too bad of Hammond. This'll annoy Jim and Stephen frightfully—drive 'em mad. [*Flinging the paper on to the settee by the piano.*] Oh, well——! [*Putting his necktie in order at the mirror.*] By Jove, we've done it at last, old lady! "House to

let,'' hey? I believe I'm keener about it than you are,
now it's come to it. What a sensation it'll cause at
" Ivanhoe," and at the Crescent! I tell you what, you
and I must have a solemn talk to-night—a parliament—
when the children have gone to bed ; a regular, serious
talk. [*Turning.*] You know, I'm still for Cheltenham.
Cheltenham seems to me to offer so many advantages.
[PHYLLIS *rises slowly.*] There's the town itself—bright
and healthy ; then the College, for Cyril. As for its
musical tastes —— [*Breaking off and looking at the
clock.*] I say, do get your things on, Phyl. [*Comparing
his watch with the clock and then timing and winding it.*]
We shall catch it if we're not punctual.

PHYLLIS.

I—I'm not going, Tad.

THADDEUS.

Not going, dear?

PHYLLIS.

No—I —— [*He advances to the right of the piano
solicitously.*] I *can't* go.

THADDEUS.

Aren't you up to it?
          [*She moves to the open window and looks into the
               garden.*

PHYLLIS.

They won't—be back—for a long while?

THADDEUS.

The children, and Trist and Helen? Not for an hour
or two.

PHYLLIS.

[*Turning.*] Tad—that girl—that girl ——

THADDEUS.

Helen?

PHYLLIS.

[*Coming forward a little.*] We're robbing her; we're robbing her. [*Shaking.*] We're all robbing her.

THADDEUS.

[*At her side.*] You've got another bad attack of nerves this afternoon—an extra bad one ——

PHYLLIS.

[*Suddenly, grasping his coat.*] Tad—I—I've broken down ——

THADDEUS.

Broken down?

PHYLLIS.

I've broken down under it.   I—I can't endure it.

THADDEUS.
[*Soothingly.*] What—what ——?

PHYLLIS.

Your brother—Edward—your brother—Edward ——

THADDEUS.

Yes?

PHYLLIS.

Everything—everything—belongs to her—Helen ——

THADDEUS.

My dear, the family were prepared to offer Helen ——

PHYLLIS.

No, no! He left every penny to her—*left* it to her.
[*Staring into his face.*] There was a will.

THADDEUS.

A will?

PHYLLIS.

I saw it.

THADDEUS.

You saw it?

PHYLLIS.

I read it—I had it in my hand ——

THADDEUS.

[*Incredulously.*] *You* did!

PHYLLIS.

Yes, I—I did away with it ——

THADDEUS.

Did away with it?

PHYLLIS.

Destroyed it.

THADDEUS.

A will—Ned's will ——! [*She turns from him and
sinks helplessly on to the settee by the fireplace. He stands
looking down upon her in a half-frightened, half-puzzled
way; then his face clears and he looks at the clock again.
Calmly.*] Phyl, I wish you'd let me have Chapman in.

PHYLLIS.

[*In a faint voice.*] No—no ——

THADDEUS.

My dear, we can afford a doctor now, if we require one. That bromide stuff he prescribed for you once—that did you no end of good. [*Going towards the door.*] I'll send Kate.

PHYLLIS.

[*Raising herself.*] Tad ——

THADDEUS.

[*Reassuringly.*] I'll stay with you till he comes.

PHYLLIS.

Tad—[*getting to her feet*] you—you think I'm not right in my head. Tad, I—I know what I'm saying. I'm telling the truth. I'm telling you the truth.

THADDEUS.

A will ——?

PHYLLIS.

[*At the round table.*] Yes—yes ——

THADDEUS.

No, no, you're talking nonsense. [*He goes to the door and there pauses, his hand on the door-knob.*] When—when ——?

PHYLLIS.

When ——?

THADDEUS.

When did you see it?

PHYLLIS.

On the—on the Wednesday night.

THADDEUS.

The Wednesday night?

PHYLLIS.

You remember—the night there **was** **no** night-nurse ——?

THADDEUS.

I remember, of course.

PHYLLIS.

Ann and Louisa had gone to the hotel to lie down, and —and I was alone with him.

THADDEUS.

I remember it all perfectly.

PHYLLIS.

[*Moving towards the ottoman, supporting herself by the table.*] I was with him from eight o'clock till nearly eleven.

THADDEUS.

Till the others came back. That was the night he—the night he sank.

PHYLLIS.

Yes ; it was just before then that he—that he ——

THADDEUS.

[*Leaving the door.*] Just before then ——?

PHYLLIS.

It was just before the change set in that he—that he sent me down-stairs.

THADDEUS.

Down-stairs?

PHYLLIS.

To the library.

THADDEUS.

The library?

PHYLLIS.

With the keys.

THADDEUS.

Keys?

PHYLLIS.

His bunch of keys.

THADDEUS.

Sent you down-stairs—to the library—with his keys?

PHYLLIS.

Yes.

THADDEUS.

What for?

PHYLLIS.

To fetch something.

THADDEUS.

Fetch something?

PHYLLIS.

From the safe.

THADDEUS.

The safe?

PHYLLIS.

The safe in the library—[*sitting on the ottoman*] the safe in the bookcase in the library.

THADDEUS.

[*Coming to her.*]   What—what did he send you to fetch, dear?

PHYLLIS.

Some—some jewelry.

THADDEUS.

Jewelry?

PHYLLIS.

Some pieces of jewelry.   He had some pieces of jewelry in his safe in the library, that he'd picked up, he said, at odd times, and he wanted to make me a present of one of them —

THADDEUS.

Make you a present ——?

PHYLLIS.

As a keepsake.   [*Her elbows on her knees, digging her fingers into her hair.*]   It was about half-past nine.   I was sitting beside his bed, thinking he was asleep, and I found him looking at me.   He recollected seeing me when I was a child, he said, skating on the ponds at Claybrook ; and he said he was sure I—I was a good wife to you—and a good mother to my children.   And then he spoke of the jewelry—and opened the drawer of the table by the bed—and took out his keys—and explained to me how to open the safe.

THADDEUS.

[*His manner gradually changing as he listens to her recital.*] You—you went down ——?

PHYLLIS.

Yes.

THADDEUS.

And—and —— ?

PHYLLIS.

And unlocked the safe. And in the lower drawer I—I came across it.

THADDEUS.

Came across —— ?

PHYLLIS.

He told me I should find four small boxes—and I could find only three—and that made me look into the drawer—and—and under a lot of other papers—I—I saw it.

THADDEUS.

*It ?*

PHYLLIS.

A big envelope, with " My Will " written upon it.
   [*There is a short silence; then he seats himself upon the settee by the piano.*

THADDEUS.

[*In a whisper.*] Well?

PHYLLIS.

[*Raising her head.*] I put it back into the drawer, and locked the safe, and went up-stairs with the jewelry. Outside the bedroom door I found Heath. I'd given him permission to run out for an hour, to get some air, with Pearce and Sadler, the housemaids. He asked me if they could do anything for me before they started. I told him no, and that Mr. Mortimore seemed brighter and stronger. I heard him going down the servant's staircase ; and then I went into the room—up to the bed —and—and he was altered.

THADDEUS.

[*Moistening his lips with his tongue.*] Ned——?

PHYLLIS.

His cheeks were more shrunken, and his jaw had dropped slightly, and his lips were quite blue ; and his breathing was short and quick. I measured the medicine which he was to have if there was any sign of collapse, and lifted him up and gave it to him. Then I rang the bell, and by and by the woman from the kitchen answered it. He was easier then—dozing, but I told her to put on her hat and jacket and go for Dr. Oswald. And then I stood watching him, and—and the idea—came to me.

THADDEUS.

The—the idea?

PHYLLIS.

My head suddenly became very clear. Every word of the argument in the train came back to me ——

THADDEUS.

Argument ?

PHYLLIS.

Between James and the others—in the train, going to Linchpool, on the Tuesday ——

THADDEUS.

Oh—oh, yes.

PHYLLIS.

If Edward died, how much would he die worth? Who
would come in for all his money? Would he remember
the family, to the extent of a mourning ring or so, in his
will? If he should die leaving *no* will! Of course Ned
would leave a will, but—where did a man's money go to
when he *didn't* leave a will?

THADDEUS.
[*Under his breath.*] To his—next-of-kin ——!

PHYLLIS.

[*Rising painfully.*] After a time, I—I went down-
stairs again. At first I persuaded myself that I only
wanted to replace the jewelry—that I didn't want to
have to explain about the jewelry to Ann and Lou;
[*moving about the room on the left*] but when I got down-
stairs I *knew* what I was going to do. And I did it as if
it was the most ordinary thing in the world. I put back
the little boxes—and took out the big envelope—and
locked up the safe again, and—read the will. [*Pausing
at the piano.*] Everything—everything—to some person
—some woman living in Paris. [*Leaning upon the piano,
a clenched hand against her brow.*] "Everything I die
possessed of to Helen Thornhill, now or late of ——"
such-and-such an address, "spinster, absolutely"; and
she was to be his executrix—"sole executrix." That
was all, except that he begged her to reward his old
servants—his old servants at his house and at the brewery.
Just a few lines—on one side of a sheet of paper ——

THADDEUS.
Written—in his own—hand?

PHYLLIS.
I think so.

THADDEUS.

You—you've seen his writing—since ——

PHYLLIS.

[*Leaving the piano.*]  Yes—I'm sure—in his own hand.

THADDEUS.

[*Heavily.*]  That clears it up, then.

PHYLLIS.

Yes.

THADDEUS.

He'd made his will—himself—himself ——

PHYLLIS.

[*Her strength failing a little.*]  Three years ago.  I—
noticed the date—[*dropping into the chair on the extreme
left*] it was three years ago ——
    [*Again there is a silence ; then he rises and walks
    about aimlessly.*

THADDEUS.

[*Trying to collect his thoughts.*]  Yes—yes ; this clears
it up.  This clears it all up.  There *was* a will.  There
*was* a will.  He *didn't* forget his child ; he didn't forget
her.  What fools—what fools we were to suppose he
*could* have forgotten his daughter !

PHYLLIS.

[*Writhing in her chair.*]  Oh, I didn't know—I didn't
guess——!  His daughter !  [*Moaning.*]  Oh ! oh !

THADDEUS.

Don't ; don't, old lady.  [*She continues her moaning.*]
Oh, don't, don't !  Let's think ; let's think, now ; let's
think.  [*He seats himself opposite to her.*]  Now, let's think.

Helen—this'll put Helen in a different position entirely ;
a different position entirely—won't it? I—I wonder—I
wonder what's the proper course for the family to take.
[*Stretching out a trembling hand to her.*] You'll have to
write down—to write down carefully—very carefully—
[*breaking off, with a change of tone*] Phyl ——

PHYLLIS.

Oh! oh!

THADDEUS.

Don't, dear, don't! Phyllis, perhaps you—didn't—·
destroy the will; not—actually—destroy it? [*Imploringly.*] You didn't destroy it, dear!

PHYLLIS.

I did—I did ——

THADDEUS.

[*Leaning back in his chair, dazed.*] I—I'm afraid—it
—it's rather—a serious matter—to—to destroy ——

PHYLLIS.

[*Starting up.*] I did destroy it; I did destroy it.
[*Pacing the room on the right.*] I kept it—I'd have burnt
it then and there if there'd been a fire—but I kept it—I
grew terrified at what I'd done—oh, I kept it till you left
me at Roper's on the Thursday morning ; and then I—I
went on to the Ford Street bridge—and tore it into pieces
—and threw them into the water. [*Wringing her hands.*]
Oh! oh!

THADDEUS.

[*His chin on his breast.*] Well—well—we've got to go
through with it. We've got—to go—through —— [*Rising
and walking about unsteadily on the left.*] Yes, yes, yes;
what a difference it'll make to everybody—not only to
Helen! What a difference it'll make at "Ivanhoe," and
at the Crescent—and to Rose ——!

PHYLLIS.

They'll curse me !   They'll curse me more than ever !

THADDEUS.

And to—to *us !*

PHYLLIS.

To us—the children —— !

THADDEUS.

[*Shaking a finger at her across the piano, cunningly.*]
Ah—ah—ah, but when the affair's really settled, we'll
still carry out our intention.   We—we'll still ——

PHYLLIS.

[*Facing him.*]  Our intention?   Our —— ?

THADDEUS.

Our intention—of leaving the town ——

PHYLLIS.

[*Wildly.*]  Leaving the town !   Oh, my God, we shall
*have* to leave the town !

THADDEUS.

[*Recoiling.*]  Oh —— !

PHYLLIS.

Leave it as beggars and outcasts !

THADDEUS.

[*Quietly.*]  Oh, yes, we shall—*have*—to leave the town
—now ——
[*The door opens and a little maid-servant enters.*
THADDEUS *looks at her with dull eyes.*

THE SERVANT.

Please, sir ——

THADDEUS.

Eh?

THE SERVANT.

Maud's just come down from "Ivanhoe." They're waiting for you.

THADDEUS.

W—waiting?

THE SERVANT.

That's the message, sir. Mr. James and the family's waiting for Mr. Thaddeus.

THADDEUS.

Oh, I —— [*Taking out his watch and fingering it.*] Yes, of course—[*to the servant*] I—I'm coming up. [*The servant withdraws.* THADDEUS *picks up his hat from the table on the left and turns to* PHYLLIS.] Good-bye, dear. [*Taking her in his arms, and kissing her, simply.*] I—I'll go up.

> [*He puts his hat on, finds his way to the door with uncertain steps, and disappears.*

**END OF THE SECOND ACT**

# THE THIRD ACT

*The scene is the dining-room in* JAMES MORTIMORE'S *house.
In the wall facing the spectator there is an arched recess with a fireplace at the back of it, and on either
side of the fireplace, within the recess, there is a chim-
ney-seat.   On the right of the recess a door opens into
the room from a hall or passage.*

*Standing out in the middle of the room is a large, oblong
dining-table, uncovered.   On the table are a couple of
inkstands, some pens, paper, and blotting-paper.   Ten
chairs are placed at regular intervals at the table—
three at each side and two at the ends.   Against the
wall on the right, near the door, stands a heavy sideboard.   On it are several pieces of ugly-looking, showy
plate, a carafe of water and a tumbler, and, upon a
tray, a decanter of red wine and some wine-glasses.
Against the same wall, but nearer to the spectator,
there is a cabinet.   In front of the cabinet there is a
round table, covered with a white cloth, on which tea-
cups and saucers are laid for ten persons.   Also on the
table are a tea-caddy and teapot, a plated kettle-stand,
a plum-cake, and other accompaniments of afternoon
tea.   On each side of the tea-table there is an armchair
belonging to the same set of chairs that surround the
dining-table.*

*Against the left-hand wall is another heavy piece of fur-
niture.   Except for this, and the sideboard and the
cabinet, the walls, below the dado rail, are bare.*

126

*The architecture, decorations, and furniture are pseudo-
artistic and vulgar. The whole suggests the home of a
common person of moderate means who has built himself
a " fine house."*

JAMES *and* STEPHEN *are seated at the further side of the
dining-table with a newspaper spread out before them.
Standing by them, reading the paper over their husbands' shoulders, are* ANN *and* LOUISA. ROSE *is sitting,
looking bored, at the right-hand end of the table, and*
PONTING, *smoking a cigar, is pacing the ·room on the
left.* LOUISA *and* ROSE, *the latter dressed in rich half-
mourning, are wearing their hats.*

JAMES.

[*Scowling at the paper.*] It's infamous.

LOUISA.

Abominable !

ANN.

It oughtn't to be allowed, James.

STEPHEN.

Ah, now James is stabbed at as well as myself.

JAMES.

The man's a blackguard ; that's what he is.

LOUISA.

His wife's a most unpleasant woman.

STEPHEN.

[*Leaning back and wiping his spectacles.*] Hitherto *I*
have been the chief object of Mr. Hammond's malice.

LOUISA.

You'll soon have your revenge now, Stephen. [*To the others.*] Stephen will soon have his revenge now.

JAMES.

By George, I've half a mind to ask Vallance to give me his opinion on this !

STEPHEN.

We might consult Vallance, certainly.

LOUISA.

And tell him what Mrs. Hammond *was.*

ANN.

When she was plain Nelly Robson.

STEPHEN.

Sssh, sssh ! Do, pray, keep the wife out of it.

PONTING.

[*Looking at his watch as he walks across to the right.*] I say, my friends, it's four o'clock, you know. [*The* MORTIMORES *stiffen themselves and regard him coldly.*] Where are these lawyer chaps?

JAMES.

[*Folding the newspaper.*] They're not in my pocket, Colonel.

STEPHEN.

No, we're not in the habit of carrying them about with us.

LOUISA.

[*Laughing sillily.*] Oh, Stephen !

ROSE.

We mustn't lose the—what's the train back, Toby?

PONTING.

[*Behind her chair, annoyed.*] Five fifty-seven.

ROSE.

I shall be dead with fatigue ; I've two parties to-night.

JAMES.

Parties ?

ROSE.

[*To* PONTING.] Destinn is singing at the Trench's, Toby.

STEPHEN.

[*Rising.*] H'm! Indeed?

ANN.

[*In an undertone, withdrawing with* LOUISA *to the fireplace.*] Singing!

JAMES.

[*Rising.*] So you're going to parties, are you, Rose? Pretty sharp work, with Ned only a month in his grave.

PONTING.

We're not conventional people.

ROSE.

[*Rising and walking away to the left.*] No, we don't mourn openly.

PONTING.

We don't carry our hearts on our what-d'ye-call-it—sleeve.

### ROSE.

And Edward wasn't in the least known in London society.

### JAMES.

[*Walking about on the right.*]  *You* knew him.

### PONTING.

[*Seating himself on the nearer side of the dining-table in the middle chair.*]  In London, my friends, reg'lar mournin' is confined to the suburbs nowadays.  May I have an ash-tray ?

### ROSE.

[*Walking about on the left.*]  And we go to Harrogate on the twenty-ninth.

### PONTING.

Good Lord, yes ; I'm kept devilish quiet *there.*
> [ANN *takes a metal ash-tray from the mantelpiece and gives it to* STEPHEN, *who almost flings it on to the table.  The door opens and a maid-servant enters followed by* ELKIN *and* VAL-LANCE.  *The lawyers carry small leather bags. The servant retires.*

### JAMES.

[*Shaking hands heartily with* ELKIN *and* VALLANCE.] Here you are !

### ELKIN.

A minute or two behind time—my fault.

### STEPHEN.

How d'ye do, Mr. Elkin ?  [*Shaking hands with* VAL-LANCE.]  Good-afternoon.

ELKIN.

[*To* PONTING.] How d'ye do?

PONTING.

[*Shortly, not rising.*] H'ah you?

VALLANCE.

[*Shaking hands with* ANN *and* LOUISA *and bowing to* ROSE.] How do you do?

ELKIN.

[*To* ROSE.] Hope you're very well, Mrs. Ponting.

ROSE.

Thanks.

VALLANCE.

[*To* PONTING, *who nods in return.*] Good-afternoon.

PONTING.

[*Bringing the palm of his hand down upon the table.*] Now, then!

JAMES.

[*To* ELKIN *and* VALLANCE, *inviting them by a gesture to be seated.*] Excuse the dining-room, gentlemen ; looks more like business than the drawing-room.

STEPHEN.

[*On the left.*] Where's Tad?

ANN.

[*Seating herself at the further side of the dining-table in the middle chair.*] Yes, where's Tad?

LOUISA.

[*Sitting beside her.*] Where are Tad and Phyllis?

JAMES.

[*Looking at his watch.*]  Five past, by my watch.

ROSE.

[*Sitting at the left-hand end of the table.*]  Oh, never mind *them*.

JAMES.

[*To* STEPHEN.]  P'r'aps you told 'em four-thirty?

STEPHEN.

[*Nettled.*]  Perhaps *I* told them!

JAMES.

All right, all right; don't flare up!  P'r'aps *I* did; there *was* a talk of making it half-past.

STEPHEN.

[*Raising his arms.*]  On the day I go to press ——

JAMES.

Ring the bell.  [*Opening the door and calling.*]  Maud! Maud ——!

> [STEPHEN *rings the bell.*  ELKIN *and* VALLANCE *are now seated,* ELKIN *in the further chair at the right-hand end of the dining-table,* VAL-LANCE *in the chair between* ELKIN *and* ANN. *They open their bags and sort and arrange their papers.*

PONTING.

We shall be here till midnight.

JAMES.

Maud ——!

ROSE.

[*Pushing her chair away from the table.*]  How vexing!

PONTING.

[*With a sneer.*] I suppose one can buy a soot of pyjamas in the town, eh, Mrs. James?

ELKIN.

*I* sha'n't detain you long.

[*The servant appears at the door.*

JAMES.

Maud, run down to Nelson Villas—just as you are ——

ROSE.

[*Satirically.*] Don't hurry them, Jim. Phyllis is smartening herself up.

STEPHEN.

[*Seating himself in the further chair at the left-hand end of the dining-table, loudly.*] Say we are waiting for Mr. Thaddeus.

JAMES.

[*To the girl.*] Mr. James and the family are waiting for Mr. Thaddeus. [*As he closes the door.*] Go along Collier Street; you may meet him.

PONTING.

[*Fussily.*] We can deal with preliminaries, at any rate. Kindly push that ash-tray a little nearer. [*To* VALLANCE.] Mr. Vallance ——

JAMES.

[*Leaving the door, resenting* PONTING'S *assumption of authority.*] I beg your pardon, Colonel; we'll give my brother another five minutes' grace, with your permission.

PONTING.

[*Shrugging his shoulders.*] By all means — ten — twenty ——

### JAMES.

[*Finding that he has the newspaper in his hand.*]  Oh—here——!  [*Opening the paper.*]  While we're waiting for Tad ——

### STEPHEN.

Ah, yes.   Read it aloud, Jim.

### PONTING.

[*Rising and moving away impatiently.*]  Tsch !

### JAMES.

Mr. Vallance—Mr. Elkin—oblige us by listening to this.   It's from the *Courier.*

### STEPHEN.

This week's *Courier*—published to-day ——

### VALLANCE.

[*To* ELKIN.]  One of our local papers.

### JAMES.

Owned by a feller o' the name of Hammond.  [*Reading.*]  "Town Topics."

### ANN.

He married a Miss Robson.

### LOUISA.

A dreadful woman.

### STEPHEN.

Sssh, sssh !   Mr. Hammond's offensive remarks are usually directed against *myself*, but in this instance——

### JAMES.

[*Walking about as he reads.*]  " A curious complication arises in connection with the estate of the late Mr. Edward Mortimore of Linchpool."

STEPHEN.

He doesn't cloak his attack, you see.

JAMES.

"As many of our readers are aware—[*running his hands over his pockets*] as many of our readers are aware——"

STEPHEN.

*He* has *made* them aware of it.

JAMES.

[*To* ANN.] Where did I put them, mother?

ANN.

[*Producing her spectacles.*] Try mine, James.
    [ANN *gives her spectacles to* STEPHEN, STEPHEN *gives them to* ROSE, *and* ROSE *presents them to* JAMES.

JAMES.

I'm getting as blear-eyed as Stephen. [*Resuming.*] "As many of our readers are aware, the whole of that gentleman's wealth passes, in consequence of his having died intestate, to a well-known Singlehampton family——"

LOUISA.

That points to us.

STEPHEN.

[*Irritably.*] Of course it does ; of course it does.

LOUISA.

There's no better-known family in Singlehampton than ours.

STEPHEN.

Sssh, sssh !

JAMES.

" —— two members of which ——"

ANN.

The Mockfords were an older family—but where *are* the Mockfords ?

JAMES.

[*To* ANN.] Give me a chance, Ann. [*Continuing.*] " —— two members of which have been for many years prominently associated with the temperance movement in this town."

STEPHEN.

[*Rising.*] My brother James and myself.

JAMES.

[*Standing at the table, facing* ELKIN *and* VALLANCE, *in his oratorical manner.*] Twelve years ago, gentlemen, I was instrumental in founding the Singlehampton and Claybrook Temperance League ——

LOUISA.

Stephen was another of the founders.

STEPHEN.

[*Joining* JAMES.] I was another.

JAMES.

And day in and day out I have devoted my best energies to furthering the objects of the League in Singlehampton *and* in Claybrook.

STEPHEN.

Very materially aided by the *Times and Mirror*, a temperance organ.

### JAMES.

And I submit that it's holding us up to ridicule and contempt—holding us up to public obloquy and derision ——

### VALLANCE.

[*To* JAMES.] What is your objection to the paragraph, Mr. Mortimore?

### JAMES.

Objection!

### ELKIN.

There's more to come, I expect.

### JAMES.

[*Grimly.*] Aye, a bit more. [*Sitting at the table.*] What d'ye think of this? [*Reading.*] "When it is remembered that the late Mr. Mortimore's fortune was derived from the brewing and the sale of *beer* ——"

### STEPHEN.

[*Sitting beside* JAMES.] The word "beer" is in italics.

### VALLANCE.

Oh, I see.

### JAMES.

" —— it will be understood that our two distinguished fellow-townsmen are placed in an extremely difficult position."

### STEPHEN.

This is the most spiteful part of it.

### JAMES.

" We have no doubt, however, that, as conscientious men, they will prove fully equal to the occasion by either renouncing their share of their late brother's property or by dedicating it entirely to the advancement of the cause they have at heart." [*Throwing the newspaper to* ELKIN *and* VALLANCE.] There it is, gentlemen.

> [*In wandering round the room,* PONTING *has come upon the decanter of wine and the wine-glasses standing on the sideboard. He is now filling a glass.*

### PONTING.

Every man has a right to his convictions. [*Taking the glass in his hand.*] A little alcohol hurts nobody ——

### JAMES.

You won't find any in *my* house.

### PONTING.

What's this, then?

### JAMES.

Currant.

### PONTING.

[*Replacing the glass, with a wry face.*] My dear Mortimore ——!

> [*He sits at the right-hand end of the table, beside* ELKIN, *and pries at the documents which* ELKIN *has taken from his bag.* VALLANCE *and* ELKIN *are reading the paragraph together,* VALLANCE *drawing his chair closer to* ELKIN'S *for that purpose.*

### JAMES.

[*To* VALLANCE.] Well, what's your opinion, Mr. Vallance? Is that libellous, or isn't it?

### STEPHEN.

Does it, or does it not, go beyond the bounds of fair comment—eh, Mr. Elkin?

VALLANCE.

[*Pacifically.*] Oh, but aren't you attaching a great deal too much importance to this ?

JAMES.

Too much ——!

ELKIN.

Why not ignore it ?

STEPHEN.

Ignore it !

VALLANCE.

Treat it as a piece of pure chaff—badinage ——

ELKIN.

In more or less bad taste.

VALLANCE.

Take no notice of it whatever.

JAMES.

[*Rising and walking away to the fireplace.*] Take no notice of it ! The townspeople will take notice of it pretty quickly.

STEPHEN.

[*Rising.*] In *my* opinion, that paragraph renders our position in the League absolutely untenable.

JAMES.

[*Standing over* VALLANCE.] Unless that paragraph is apologized for, withdrawn ——

STEPHEN.

[*Standing over* ELKIN.] Explained away ——

JAMES.

Aye, explained away ——

VALLANCE.

I don't see how it can be explained away.

ELKIN.

[*Dryly.*] The proposition is a perfectly accurate one, whatever you may think of the corollary.

VALLANCE.

You *are* ardent advocates of temperance.

ELKIN

Your late brother's property *was* amassed mainly by beer.

VALLANCE.

It can hardly be explained away.

STEPHEN.

[*Walking to the left.*] Good heavens above, I've ex-plained things away often enough in *my* paper!

JAMES.

[*Coming forward on the right.*] This does us at the League, then—*does* us; knocks our influence into a cocked hat.

ELKIN.

[*To* JAMES *and* STEPHEN, *while* VALLANCE *folds the paper.*] After all, gentlemen, when you come to reflect upon it, the laugh is with *you.*

JAMES.

*Is* it?

ELKIN.

[*Genially.*] The *Courier* has its little joke, but *you've* got the money, remember.

JAMES.

Oh, that's true.

STEPHEN.

[*Walking about on the left.*] That's true ; that's true.

JAMES.

[*Walking about on the right, rattling his loose cash.*] Aye, *we've* got the mopuses.

ROSE.

[*Tilting her chair on its hind legs.*] I say, Jim—Stephen —why don't you two boys, between you, present the League with a handsome hall ——?

JAMES.

[*Pausing in his walk.*] Hall ?

ROSE.

Build the temperance folk a meeting-place of their own —a headquarters ——

PONTING.

[*Mischievously.*] He, he, he ! That 'ud smooth 'em down. Capital idea, Rosie !

JAMES *and* STEPHEN.

We !

JAMES.

I'd see 'em damned first. [*To the ladies.*] I beg pardon ——

ANN.

[*With unusual animation.*] No, no ; you're quite right, James.

STEPHEN.

[*At the fireplace.*] That would be playing into Mr. Hammond's hands with a vengeance.

JAMES.

[*Walking across to the left, derisively.*] Ha! Wouldn't Hammond crow, hey! Ha, ha, ha!

STEPHEN.

No, if the situation becomes too acute—painful as it would be to me—I shall resign.

JAMES.

[*Determinedly.*] Resign.

STEPHEN.

Sever my connection with the League.

JAMES.

Leave 'em to swill themselves with their lemonade and boiled tea —— !

STEPHEN.

[*Coming forward on the right.*] And to find out how they get on without us.

JAMES.

Serve 'em up in their own juice !

STEPHEN.

[*Meeting* JAMES *in the middle of the room on the nearer side of the dining-table.*] You know, Jim, we've never gone *quite* so far—you and I—with the principles of temperance as some.

JAMES.

[*Eyeing him curiously.*] Never gone so far ——?

STEPHEN.

As old Bob Amphlett, for example—never.

JAMES.

Oh, yes, we have, and a deuced sight further.

STEPHEN.

Excuse me—I've *always* been for moderation rather than for total abstinence.

JAMES.

Have yer? [*Walking away to the left.*] First I've heard of it.

STEPHEN.

Anyhow, a man may broaden his views with years and experience. [*Argumentatively.*] Take the hygienic aspect of the case. Only the other day, Sir Vincent West, probably the ablest physician in England ——

LOUISA.

[*Abruptly.*] Stephen ——!

STEPHEN.

[*Angrily.*] Don't interrupt me.

LOUISA.

[*With energy, rising.*] I've maintained it throughout my life—it's nothing new from my lips ——

STEPHEN.

What ——?

LOUISA.

There are two sides to every question.

STEPHEN.

[*Hurrying round the table to join* LOUISA.]  Exactly— exactly—as Lou says ——

LOUISA.

It's been almost a second religion with me.  I've preached it in season and out of season ——

STEPHEN.

[*With conviction.*]  There *are* two sides ——

LOUISA.

Two sides to every question.

JAMES.

[*To* ANN, *pointing to the door.*]  Mother—— [*The door has been opened by another maid-servant, who carries a tray on which are a plated kettle, a dish of toast, and a plentiful supply of bread-and-butter.  The girl remains in the doorway.  ANN rises and goes to her and takes the kettle from the tray.  JAMES comes forward and seats himself on the nearer side of the dining-table in the middle chair.*]  Look here ; I don't wait another minute for the Tads—not a second.

PONTING.

Ah !

      [LOUISA *follows* ANN *and takes the toast and the bread-and-butter from the servant, who then disappears, closing the door.*

STEPHEN.

[*Again sitting in the further chair at the left-hand end of the dining-table.*]  Inexcusable of them—inexcusable.
      [ANN *and* LOUISA *come to the tea-table and, draw- ing the two armchairs up to it, seat themselves*

*and prepare the tea. The kettle is set upon the stand, the spirit-lamp is lighted,* ANN *measures the tea from the caddy into the pot, and* LOUISA *cuts the plum-cake.*

JAMES.

Mr. Elkin—Mr. Vallance ——

PONTING.

Now, Mr. Vallance ; now, Mr. Elkin !

ELKIN.

[*To* VALLANCE.] Will you —— ?

VALLANCE.

No, no—you ——

ELKIN.

Well, gentlemen—[*to* ROSE] Mrs. Ponting—Mr. Vallance and I have to report to you that we've received no communication of any kind in answer to our circulars and advertisements ——

JAMES.

[*To* ANN, *who is making a clatter with the kettle.*] Steady, mother !

PONTING.

[*To the ladies at the tea-table.*] Sssh, sssh, sssh !

ELKIN.

No communication from any solicitor who has pre-'pared a will for your late brother, nor from anybody who has knowingly witnessed a will executed by him.

STEPHEN.

Mr. Vallance has apprised us of this already.

JAMES.

[*Raising a hand.*]  Order!   There's a formal way of doing things and a lax way.

STEPHEN.

I merely mentioned ——
     [PONTING *raps the table sharply with his knuckles.*

ELKIN.

I may say that, in addition to the issuing of the circulars and advertisements, I have made search in every place I could think of, and have inquired of every person likely to be of help in the matter.   In fact, I've taken every possible step to find, or trace, a will.

VALLANCE.

Without success.

ELKIN.

Without success.

JAMES.

[*Magnanimously.*]  And *I* say that the family bears no grudge to Mr. Elkin for doing his duty.

STEPHEN.

[*In the same spirit.*]  Hear, hear!

PONTING.

[*Testily.*]  Of course not ; of course not.

ROSE.

It's all the more satisfactory, it seems to me, that he *has* worried round.

JAMES.

The family *thanks* Mr. Elkin.

###### STEPHEN.
We thank Mr. Elkin.

###### ELKIN.
[*After a stiff inclination of the head.*] The only other observation I wish to make is that several gentlemen employed in the office of the brewery in Linchpool have at different times witnessed the late Mr. Mortimore's signature to documents which have apparently required the attestation of two witnesses.

###### PONTING.
[*Curtly.*] That amounts to nothing.

###### JAMES.
There are a good many documents, aren't there, where two witnesses are required to a signature?

###### ELKIN.
Deeds under seal, certainly.

###### STEPHEN.
I remember having to sign, some years ago ——
          [PONTING *again raps the table.*

###### VALLANCE.
But none of these gentlemen at the brewery can recall that any particular document appeared to him to be a will, which is not a document under seal.

###### JAMES.
Besides, a man signing a will always tells the witnesses that it *is* his will they're witnessing, doesn't he, Mr. Vallance?

###### VALLANCE.
A solicitor would, in the ordinary course of practice,

inform the witnesses to a will of the nature of the document they were attesting, undoubtedly.

ELKIN.

Granted ; but a testator, supposing he were executing his will in his own house or office, and not in the presence of a solicitor, is under no legal necessity to do so, and may omit to do so.

JAMES.

[*Rolling about in his chair.*] Oh, well, we needn't——

PONTING.

[*Looking at his watch.*] In heaven's name——!

STEPHEN.

We needn't go into all this.

ELKIN.

No, no ; I simply draw attention to the point. [*Unfolding a document.*] Well, gentlemen—Mrs. Ponting—this is a statement—[*handing another document to* VALLANCE] here is a copy of it, Mr. Vallance—this is a statement of particulars of stocks, shares, and other items of estate, with their values at the death of the late Mr. Mortimore, and a schedule of the debts so far as they are known to me.

> [*There is a general movement.* JAMES *rises and goes to* VALLANCE. STEPHEN *also rises, stretching out an eager hand towards* VALLANCE. ROSE *draws nearer to the table,* PONTING *still closer to* ELKIN. ANN *and* LOUISA, *too, show a disposition to desert the tea-table.*

JAMES.

[*To* ANN, *as he passes her.*] You get on with the tea, mother. [*To* VALLANCE.] Allow me, Mr. Vallance——

[V<small>ALLANCE</small> *gives him the duplicate of the state-*
*ment.*

P<small>ONTING</small>.

What's it come out at ; what's it come out at ?

S<small>TEPHEN</small>.

What's it come out at ?

R<small>OSE</small>.

Yes, what does it come out at ?  Jim ——

S<small>TEPHEN</small>.

Jim ——

[J<small>AMES</small> *joins* S<small>TEPHEN</small> *and they examine the dupli-*
*cate together.*  R<small>OSE</small> *rises and endeavors to read*
*it with them.*

E<small>LKIN</small>.

I estimate the gross value of the estate, which, as you
will see, consists entirely of personal property, at one
hundred and ninety-two thousand pounds.

P<small>ONTING</small>.

The *gross* value.

S<small>TEPHEN</small>.

Yes, but what do *we* get ?

P<small>ONTING</small> *and* R<small>OSE</small>.

What do *we* get ?

J<small>AMES</small>.

After all deductions.

E<small>LKIN</small>.

Roughly speaking, after payment of debts, death
duties, and expenses, there will be about a hundred and

seventy thousand pounds to divide. [*Those who are standing sit again.* James *seats himself next to* Stephen *and, with pen and ink, they make calculations on paper.* Ponting *does the same.* Rose, *closing her eyes, fans herself happily, and the two ladies at the tea-table resume their preparations with beaming countenances.* Elkin *leans back in his chair.*] Mr. Vallance ——

### Vallance.

[*To* Rose, James, *and* Stephen.] Mrs. Ponting and gentlemen—[Ponting *raps the table and* James *and* Stephen *look up*] I advise you that, as next-of-kin of the late Mr. Mortimore, if you are satisfied—and in my opinion you may reasonably be satisfied—that he died intestate—I advise you that any one or more of you, not exceeding three, [*the door opens quietly and* Thaddeus *appears. He is very pale, but is outwardly calm. After a look in the direction of the table, he closes the door*] may apply for Letters of Administration of your late brother's estate. It isn't necessary or usual, however, I may tell you, to have more than one administrator, and I suggest ——

> [*Hearing the click of the lock as* Thaddeus *shuts the door, everybody turns and glances at him.*

### Rose.

[*Opening her eyes.*] Here's Tad.

### Stephen.

[*Grumpily.*] Oh ——

### Rose.

[*Tossing* Thaddeus *a greeting.*] Hallo !

### James.

[*To* Thaddeus, *with a growl.*] Oh, you've arrived.

STEPHEN.

[*To* THADDEUS.] Did I say four or half-past ——?

LOUISA.

Where's Phyllis?

ANN.

Where's Phyllis?

THADDEUS.

[*In a low voice, advancing.*] She—she didn't feel well
enough ——
　　　　　[PONTING *raps the inkstand with his penholder.*

JAMES.

[*Pointing to the chair beside him, imperatively.*] Sit
down; sit down. [THADDEUS *sits, his elbows on the table,
his eyes cast down.*] Mr. Vallance ——

VALLANCE.

[*To* THADDEUS.] Good-afternoon, Mr. Mortimore.

ELKIN.

[*Nodding to* THADDEUS.] How d'ye do?

THADDEUS.

[*Almost inaudibly.*] Good-afternoon.

VALLANCE.

[*To the others.*] I suppose we needn't go back ——?

A MURMUR.

No, no; no, no.

JAMES.

[*Pushing the duplicate of the statement under* THAD-
DEUS'S *eyes.*] A hundred and seventy thousand pound to
divide.

###### STEPHEN.

A hundred and seventy thousand.

###### PONTING.

[*Finishing his sum.*] Forty-two thousand five hundred apiece.

###### VALLANCE.

[*Resuming.*] I was saying that it isn't usual to have more than one administrator, and I was about to suggest that the best course will be for you, Mr. James, to act in that capacity, and for you, Mr. Stephen, and you, Mr. Thaddeus, or one of you, and Colonel Ponting, to be the sureties to the bond for the due administration of the estate.

###### JAMES.

[*Cheerfully.*] I'm in your hands, Mr. Vallance.

###### STEPHEN.

I'm agreeable.

###### PONTING.

And I.

###### VALLANCE.

The procedure is this—perhaps I'd better explain it. [*Producing a form of " Oath for Administrators " which is among his papers.*] The intended administrator will make an affidavit stating when and where the deceased died, that he died intestate, [THADDEUS *looks up*] a bachelor without a parent, and that the deponent is a natural and lawful brother and one of the next-of-kin of the deceased ——

###### THADDEUS.

[*Touching* VALLANCE'S *arm.*] Mr. Vallance ——

VALLANCE.

Eh?

THADDEUS.

We—we mustn't go on with this.

VALLANCE.

I beg pardon?

THADDEUS.

The family mustn't go on with this.

VALLANCE.

Mustn't go on ——?

JAMES.

[*To* THADDEUS.] What a'yer talking about?

THADDEUS.

[*After a hurried look round.*] There—there was **a** will.

VALLANCE.

A will?

THADDEUS.

He—he made a will.

JAMES.

*Who* did?

THADDEUS.

Edward. He—he left a will.

JAMES.

[*Roughly.*] What the —— !

ELKIN.

[*To* JAMES, *interrupting him.*] One moment.   Your brother has something to say to us, Mr. Mortimore.

STEPHEN.

What—what's he mean by ——?

ELKIN.

[*To* STEPHEN.] Please—[*To* THADDEUS.]   Yes, sir ? [THADDEUS *is silent.*] *What* about a will ? [THADDEUS *is still silent.*]   Eh ?

THADDEUS.

I—I saw it.

ELKIN.

Saw a will ?

THADDEUS.

I—I opened it—I—I read it ——

ELKIN.

Read it ?

THADDEUS.

I—tore it up—got rid of it.
         [*Again there is silence, the* MORTIMORES *and the* PONTINGS *sitting open-mouthed and motionless.*

ELKIN.

[*After a while.*] Mr. Vallance, I think we ought to tell Mr. Mortimore that he appears to be making a confession of the gravest kind ——

VALLANCE.

Yes.

### ELKIN.

One that puts him in a very serious position.

### VALLANCE.

[*To* THADDEUS, *after a further pause.*] Mr. Morti-more ——?

[THADDEUS *makes no response.*

### ELKIN.

If, understanding that, he chooses to continue, there is nothing to prevent our hearing him.

### THADDEUS.

[*Looking straight before him, his arms still upon the table, locking and unlocking his hands as he speaks.*] It—it happened on the Wednesday night—in Cannon Row—in Ned's house—the night before he died—the night we were left without a nurse. [*Another pause.* VALLANCE *takes a sheet of paper and selects a pen.* ELKIN *pushes the inkstand nearer to him.*] Mrs. James—and—and Mrs. Stephen—my—my sisters-in-law ——

[ANN *and* LOUISA *get to their feet and advance a step or two.*

### ELKIN.

[*Hearing the rustle of their skirts and turning to them.*] Keep your seats, ladies, please.

[*They sit again, drawing their chairs close together.*

### THADDEUS.

My sisters-in-law had gone home—that is, to their hotel—to get a few hours' sleep in case of their having to sit up through the night. Jim and Stephen and I were out and about, trying to find a night-nurse who'd take Nurse Ralston's place temporarily. At about nine o'clock, I looked in at Cannon Row, to see how things were getting on.

### VALLANCE.

[*Who is writing.*] The Wednesday? Mr. Edward Mortimore dying on Thursday, the twentieth of June ——

### ELKIN.

On the morning of Thursday, the twentieth.

### VALLANCE.

That makes the Wednesday we are speaking of, Wednesday, June the nineteenth.

### ELKIN.

[*To* THADDEUS.] You looked in at Cannon Row —— ?

### VALLANCE.

At about nine o'clock on the night of Wednesday, June the nineteenth.

### THADDEUS.

I—I went up-stairs and sat by Ned's bed, and by and by he began talking to me about—about Phyllis. He—he'd taken rather a fancy to her, he said, and he wanted to give her a memento—a keepsake.

### ELKIN.

Phyllis——?

### VALLANCE.

[*To* ELKIN.] His wife. [*To* THADDEUS.] Your wife?
[THADDEUS *nods.*

### ELKIN.

[*Recollecting.*] Of course.

### THADDEUS.

[*Moistening his lips with his tongue.*] He—he had some little bits of jewelry in his safe, and he—he asked me to go down-stairs and—and to bring them up to him.

ELKIN.

[*Keenly.*] In his safe?

VALLANCE.

The safe in the library?

[THADDEUS *nods again.*

ELKIN.

Quite so.

VALLANCE.

And—er ——?

THADDEUS.

He—he gave me his keys, and I—I went down—I ——
[*He stops suddenly and* VALLANCE *glances at him.
Noticing his extreme pallor,* VALLANCE *looks
round the room. Seeing the water-bottle upon
the sideboard,* VALLANCE *rises and fills the
tumbler. Returning to the table, he places the
glass before* THADDEUS *and resumes his seat.*

THADDEUS.

[*After a gulp of water.*] It was—it was in the drawer
of the safe—the drawer ——

ELKIN.

What was?

THADDEUS.

[*Wiping his mouth with his handkerchief.*] A large
envelope—a large envelope—the envelope containing the
will.

VALLANCE.

How did you know ——?

THADDEUS.

" My Will " was written on it.

VALLANCE.

[*Writing.*]  " My Will "——

ELKIN.

On the envelope? [THADDEUS *nods.*]  You say you opened it?

[THADDEUS *nods.*

VALLANCE.

Opened the envelope ——

ELKIN.

And inside—you found —— ?

VALLANCE.

What did you find?

THADDEUS.

Ned's will.

VALLANCE.

[*Writing.*]  What appeared to be your brother Edward's will.

ELKIN.

You read it? [THADDEUS *nods.*]  You recollect who was interested under it? [THADDEUS *nods.*]  Will you tell us —— ?

[*The* MORTIMORES *and the* PONTINGS *crane their necks forward, listening breathlessly.*

THADDEUS.

He left everything—[*taking another gulp of water*] everything—to Miss Thornhill.

[*There is a slight, undecided movement on the part of the* MORTIMORES *and the* PONTINGS.

ELKIN.

[*Calmly but firmly.*] Keep your seats; keep your seats, *please*. [*To* THADDEUS.] Can you recall the general form of the will?

THADDEUS.

[*Straining his memory.*] Everything he had—died possessed of—to Helen Thornhill—spinster—of some address in Paris—absolutely. And—and he appointed her his sole executrix.

ELKIN.

Do you recollect the date?

THADDEUS.

Date ——?

ELKIN.

Did you observe the date of the will?

THADDEUS.

[*Quickly.*] Oh, yes; it was made three years ago.

ELKIN.

[*To* VALLANCE.] When she came of age.

THADDEUS.

Oh, and he asked her to remember his servants—old servants at the brewery and in Cannon Row. [*Leaning back, exhausted.*] There was nothing else. It was very short—written by Ned ——

ELKIN.

The whole of it? [THADDEUS *nods, with half-closed eyes.*] The whole of it was in his handwriting? [THAD-

DEUS *nods again.*] Ah! [*To* VALLANCE, *with a note of triumph in his voice.*] A holograph will, Mr. Vallance, prepared by the man himself.

### VALLANCE.

[*Now taking up the questioning of* THADDEUS.] Tell me, Mr. Mortimore—have you any exact recollection as to whether this document, which you describe as a will, was duly signed and witnessed?

### THADDEUS.

[*Rousing himself.*] It was—it was—signed by Ned.

### VALLANCE.

Was it signed, not only by your brother, but by two witnesses under an attestation clause stating that the testator signed in the joint presence of those witnesses and that each of them signed in his presence?

### THADDEUS.

I—I don't recollect that.

### VALLANCE.

[*Writing.*] You've no recollection of that.
[JAMES, STEPHEN, *and* PONTING *stir themselves.*

### JAMES.

[*Hoarsely.*] He doesn't recollect that, Mr. Vallance.

### STEPHEN.

[*In quavering tones.*] No, he—he doesn't recollect that.

### PONTING.

[*Pulling at his moustache with trembling fingers.*] That's most important, Mr. Vallance, isn't it—isn't it?

VALLANCE.

[*To* THADDEUS, *not heeding the interruption.*] You say you destroyed this document——

ELKIN.

Tore it up.

VALLANCE.

When—and where? In the room—in the library?

THADDEUS.

[*Thinking.*] N-no—out of doors.

VALLANCE.

Out of doors. When?

THADDEUS.

[*At a loss.*] When —— ?

VALLANCE.

When. [*Looking at him in surprise.*] You can't remember —— ?

THADDEUS.

[*Recollecting.*] Oh, yes, yes, yes, yes. Some time between ten and eleven on the Thursday morning, after I left Phyllis—after I left my wife at Roper's to be measured for her black.

VALLANCE.

[*Writing.*] What did you do then?

THADDEUS.

[*Readily.*] I went to Ford Street bridge, and tore up the paper, and dropped the pieces into the Linch.

VALLANCE.

[*Writing.*] Into the river——

ELKIN.

One more question, Mr. Mortimore—to make your motive perfectly clear to us. May we assume that, on the night of June the nineteenth, you were sufficiently acquainted with the law of intestacy to know that, if this dying man left no will, you would be likely to benefit considerably?

THADDEUS.

Well, I—I had—the idea ——

ELKIN.

The idea?

THADDEUS.

I—I —— [*Recollecting.*] Oh, yes ; there'd been a discussion in the train, you see, on the Tuesday, going to Linchpool ——

ELKIN.

Discussion?

THADDEUS.

Among us all, as to how a man's money is disposed of, if he dies intestate.

ELKIN.

[*Nodding.*] Precisely. [*To* JAMES *and* STEPHEN.] You remember that conversation taking place, gentlemen?

JAMES.

Oh, I—I dessay.

ELKIN.

[*To* THADDEUS.] So that, when you came upon the envelope with the endorsement upon it—" My Will " —— ?

THADDEUS.

[*Leaning his head upon his hands.*] Yes—yes ——

VALLANCE.

[*Running his eyes over his notes, to* THADDEUS.] Have
you anything to add, Mr. Mortimore?

THADDEUS.

[*In a muffled voice.*] No. [*Quickly.*] Oh, there is one
thing I should like to add. [*Brokenly.*] With regard to
Miss Thornhill—I—I hope you'll bear in mind that I—
that none of us—heard from Mr. Elkin of the existence
of a child—a daughter—till the Thursday—middle-
day ——

ELKIN.

That is so.

THADDEUS.

It doesn't make it much better; only—a girl—alone in
the world—one wouldn't—[*breaking off*] no, I've nothing more to say.

ELKIN.

[*To* THADDEUS.] And we may take it that your present act, Mr. Mortimore, is an act of conscience, purely?
[THADDEUS *inclines his head. There is silence
again, the* MORTIMORES *and the* PONTINGS
*presenting a picture of utter wretchedness. The
ladies' tears begin to flow.*

JAMES.

[*After a time, speaking with some difficulty.*] Well ——

STEPHEN.

[*Piteously.*] Mr. Vallance ——?

JAMES.

What—what's to be done, Mr. Vallance?

PONTING.

[*To the ladies.*] For God's sake, be quiet!

JAMES.

[*A clenched fist on the table.*] What we want to know is—what we want to know is—who does my brother Edward's money belong to now—*her* or us?

STEPHEN.

[*In agony.*] Her!

PONTING.

Don't be a damn fool, Mortimore!

VALLANCE.

Well, gentlemen, I confess I am hardly prepared to express an opinion off-hand on the legal aspect of the case ——

PONTING.

The will's torn up—it's destroyed ——!

STEPHEN.

It's destroyed—gone—gone!

PONTING.

Gone.

VALLANCE.

But I need not remind you, there is another aspect——

PONTING.

I don't care a rap for any other aspect——

STEPHEN.

We want the *law* explained to us—the law ———

PONTING.

The law —— !

JAMES.

[*To* ELKIN.] Mr. Elkin ——?

ELKIN.

You appeal to me, gentlemen ?

STEPHEN *and* PONTING.

Yes—yes ——

ELKIN.

Then I feel bound to tell you that *I* shall advise Miss Thornhill, as the executrix named in the will, to apply to the Court for probate of its substance and effect ——

VALLANCE.

[*To* ELKIN.] Ask the Court to presume the will to have been made in due form ——?

ELKIN.

Decidedly.

> [STEPHEN *and* PONTING *fall back in their seats in a stupor, and once more there is silence, broken only by the sound of the women sniveling.* ELKIN *and* VALLANCE *slowly proceed to collect their papers.*

JAMES.

[*Turning upon* THADDEUS, *brutally.*] Have you—have you told Phyllis—have you told your wife what you've been up to?

[*At the mention of* PHYLLIS, *there is a movement of indignation on the part of the ladies.*

ROSE.

Ha!

JAMES.

[*To* THADDEUS.]  Have yer?

THADDEUS.

Y-yes—just before I came out.  [*Weakly.*]  That—that's what made me so late.

JAMES.

[*Between his teeth.*]  What does *she* think of yer?

THADDEUS.

Oh, she—she's dreadfully—cut up—of course.

ROSE.

[*Hysterically.*]  The jewelry!  Ha, ha, ha!  [*Rising.*] She's managed to get hold of some of the jewelry, at any rate.

ANN.

[*With a sob.*]  Yes, she—she managed *that.*

LOUISA.

[*Mopping her face.*]  She's kept that from us artfully enough.

ROSE.

[*Going over to* ANN *and* LOUISA, *who rise to receive her.*]  Ha, ha!  Edward's "little bits" of jewelry!

ANN.

Little bits!

ROSE.

They're little bits that are *left*.

LOUISA.

How many did she have of them, I wonder!

ROSE.

She shall be made to restore them ——

LOUISA.

Every one of them.

THADDEUS.

No, no, no —— [*Stretching out a hand towards the ladies.*] Rosie—Ann—Lou—Phyllis hadn't any of the jewelry—not a scrap. I put it all back into the safe. I —I swear she hadn't any of it.

ELKIN.

Why did you do that?

THADDEUS.

[*Agitatedly.*] Why, you see, Mr. Elkin, when I carried it up-stairs, I found my brother Edward in a state of collapse—a sort of faint ——

ELKIN.

[*With a nod.*] Ah ——

THADDEUS.

And Phyllis—my wife—she sent me off at once for the doctor. It was on the Wednesday evening, you know ——

VALLANCE.

[*Pricking up his ears.*] Your wife, Mr. Mortimore ——?

THADDEUS.

It was on the Wednesday evening that the change set in.

VALLANCE.

[*To* THADDEUS.] Your wife sent you off at once —— ?

THADDEUS.

[*To* VALLANCE.] To fetch the doctor.

VALLANCE.

[*Raising his eyebrows.*] Oh, Mrs. Mortimore was in the house while all this was going on?

THADDEUS.

Y-yes; she was left in charge of him—in charge of Ned——

ELKIN.

[*To* VALLANCE, *in explanation.*] To allow these other ladies to rest, preparatory to their taking charge later.

THADDEUS.

Yes.

VALLANCE.

I hadn't gathered ——

JAMES.

[*Who had been sitting glaring into space, thoughtfully.*] Hold hard. [*To* THADDEUS.] *You* didn't go for the doctor.

THADDEUS.

Yes, I—I went——

STEPHEN.

[*Awakening from his trance.*] Phyllis sent the cook for the doctor.

THADDEUS.

Yes, yes ; you're quite right. The cook was the first to go ——

ELKIN.

[*To* THADDEUS.] You followed?

THADDEUS.

I followed.

JAMES.

[*Knitting his brows.*] It must have been a good time afterwards.

THADDEUS.

Y-yes, perhaps it was.

JAMES.

I was at Dr. Oswald's when the woman arrived. The doctor was out, and ——

VALLANCE.

[*To* THADDEUS.] You said your wife sent you at once.

THADDEUS.

Told me to go at once. There—there was the jewelry to put back into the safe ——

VALLANCE.

[*Eyeing* THADDEUS.] What time was it when you *got* to the doctor's?

THADDEUS.

Oh—ten, I should say—or a quarter-past.

JAMES.

[*Shaking his head.*] No. I sat there, waiting for Dr. Oswald to come in ——

STEPHEN.

[*To* THADDEUS.] Besides, that couldn't have been ; you were with me then.

JAMES.

[*To* STEPHEN.] Was he ?

STEPHEN.

Why, yes; he and I were at the Nurses' Home in Wharton Street from half-past nine till ten.

JAMES.

Half-past nine —— ?

STEPHEN.

[*Becoming more confident as he proceeds.*] And we never left each other till we went back to Cannon Row.

VALLANCE.

Let us understand this ——

PONTING.

[*Who has gradually revived, eagerly.*] Yes—yes—[*to the ladies*] Sssh !

STEPHEN.

And, what's more, we allowed ourselves a quarter of an hour to walk to Wharton Street.

JAMES.

[*Quietly, looking round.*] Hallo ——!

THADDEUS.

It—it's evident that I—that I'm mistaken in thinking that I—that I went to Dr. Oswald's ——

VALLANCE.

Mistaken?

THADDEUS.

I—I suppose that, as the woman had already gone, I—I considered it—wasn't necessary —— [*To* ELKIN *and* VALLANCE, *passing his hand before his eyes.*] You must excuse my stupidity, gentlemen.

VALLANCE.

[*To* THADDEUS, *distrustfully.*] Then, according to your brother Stephen, Mr. Mortimore, you were in Cannon Row, on the occasion of this particular visit, no longer than from nine o'clock till a quarter-past?

STEPHEN.

Not so long, because we met, by arrangement, at a quarter-past nine, in the hall of the Grand Hotel ——

JAMES.

The hotel's six or seven minutes' walk from Cannon Row ——

PONTING.

Quite, quite.

THADDEUS.

[*A little wildly.*] I said I called in at Cannon Row at *about* nine o'clock. It may have been half-past eight ; it may have been eight ——

JAMES.

Ann and Lou didn't leave Cannon Row till past eight ——

LOUISA.

[*Standing, with* ANN *and* ROSE, *by the tea-table.*] It had gone eight ——

JAMES.

I walked 'em round to the Grand ——

STEPHEN.

The *three* of us walked with them to the Grand ——!

LOUISA.

All three ——

JAMES.

So we did.

STEPHEN.

[*Excitedly.*] And then Thaddeus went off to the Clarence Hospital with a note from Dr. Oswald——

JAMES.

By George, yes!

STEPHEN.

I left him opposite the Exchange—it must have been nearly half-past eight *then* ——!

> [JAMES *rises. The ladies draw nearer to the dining-table.*

THADDEUS.

Ah, but I didn't go to the hospital—I didn't go to the hospital ——

STEPHEN.

[*Rising.*] Yes, you did. You brought a note *back* from the hospital, for us to take to Wharton Street——

**VALLANCE.**

[*To* ELKIN.] How far is the Clarence Hospital from the Exchange?

**ELKIN.**

A ten minutes' drive. It's on the other side of the water.

**THADDEUS.**

I—I—I'd forgotten the hospital ——

**JAMES.**

[*Scowling at* THADDEUS.] Forgotten ——?

**THADDEUS.**

I—I—I mean I—I thought the hospital came later—after I'd been to Wharton Street ——

**JAMES.**

[*Going to* VALLANCE *and tapping him on the shoulder.*] Mr. Vallance ——

**THADDEUS.**

I—I must have gone to Cannon Row *between* my return from the hospital and my meeting Stephen at the Grand ——

**JAMES.**

[*To* ELKIN *and* VALLANCE.] Why, he couldn't have *done* it, gentlemen ——

**PONTING.**

Impossible !

**STEPHEN.**

It's obvious ; he *couldn't* have done it.

THADDEUS.

I—I was only a few minutes at the hospital——

ELKIN.

[*Scribbling on the back of a document.*] Oh, yes, he could have done it—barely ——

VALLANCE.

[*Making a mental calculation.*] Assuming that he left his brother at the Exchange at eight-twenty ——

ELKIN.

Ten minutes *to* the hospital.

VALLANCE.

If he drove there ——

THADDEUS.

I did drive—I did drive ——

PONTING.

[*Who is also figuring it out on paper.*] Ten minutes back ——

ELKIN.

Ten minutes *at* the hospital ——

PONTING.

Eight-fifty ——

THADDEUS.

Eight-fifty in Cannon Row! That was it—that was it, Mr. Elkin ——

JAMES.

Give him twenty minutes in Cannon Row—*give* it him! He couldn't have done all he says he did in the time, gentlemen ——

STEPHEN.

He couldn't have *done* it ——

PONTING.

Impossible !

ELKIN.

[*To* PONTING.] No, no, please—not impossible.

VALLANCE.

[*To* STEPHEN.] When you met Mr. Thaddeus Morti-more—you—when you met him in the hall of the Grand Hotel, before starting for Wharton Street, did he say any-thing to you as to his having just called at the house —— ?

STEPHEN.

No.

VALLANCE.

Nothing as to an alarming change in your brother's condition ?

STEPHEN.

Not a syllable.

JAMES.

[*To* ELKIN *and* VALLANCE.] Oh, there's a screw loose here, gentlemen, surely ?

STEPHEN.

[*Joining* JAMES.] That is *most* extraordinary, Mr. Vallance—isn't it ? Not a syllable !
> [ANN *and* LOUISA *join their husbands and the four
> gather round* ELKIN *and* VALLANCE. ROSE
> *stands behind* PONTING'S *chair.*

THADDEUS.

You see—Edward—Edward had rallied before I left Cannon Row.   He—he'd fallen into a nice, quiet sleep——

JAMES.

All in twenty minutes, gentlemen—twenty minutes at the outside !

VALLANCE.

[*To* THADDEUS.]  Mr. Mortimore ——

ANN.

I remember ——

PONTING.

[*To* ANN.]  Hold your tongue !

VALLANCE.

Mr. Mortimore, *who let you into the house* in Cannon Row on the night of June the nineteenth —— ?

PONTING.

Ah, yes ——

VALLANCE.

At *any* time between the hours of eight o'clock —— ?

STEPHEN.

And eleven.

ELKIN.

[*To* THADDEUS.]  Who gave you admittance—which of the servants ?

THADDEUS.

I—I can't—I don't—[*blankly, addressing* VALLANCE] was it the—the butler —— ?

### VALLANCE.

No, no; I ask *you.* [*To* ELKIN, *who nods in reply.*] Have you the servants' addresses ?

### THADDEUS.

But you wouldn't—you wouldn't trust to the servants' memories as to—as to which of them opened the front door to me a month ago ! [*With an attempt at a laugh.*] It's ridiculous !

### ELKIN.

[*Reprovingly.*] Ah, now, now, Mr. Mortimore !

### THADDEUS.

[*Starting up from the table.*] Oh, it isn't fair—it isn't fair of you to badger me like this ; it isn't fair !

### VALLANCE.

Nobody desires to " badger " you ——

### THADDEUS.

Trip me up, then—confuse me. [*At the left-hand end of the table, clutching the back of a chair.*] The will—the will's the main point—Ned's will. What does it matter—what can it matter, to a quarter of an hour or so—when I was in Cannon Row, or how long I was there ? One would think, by the way I'm being treated, gentlemen, that I'd something to gain by this, instead of everything to lose—everything to lose !

### JAMES.

[*Coming forward, on the further side of the table.*] Don't you whine about what *you've* got to lose —— !

### STEPHEN.

[*Joining him.*] What about *us !*

### THE LADIES.

Us !

### PONTING.

[*Hitting the table.*]  Yes, confound you !

### VALLANCE.

Colonel Ponting ——— !

### ELKIN.

[ *To* JAMES *and* STEPHEN.]  It seems to me—if my friend Mr. Vallance will allow me to say so—that you are really bearing a little hardly on your brother Thaddeus.

### THADDEUS.

[*Gratefully.*]  Thank you, Mr. Elkin.

### ELKIN.

What reason—what possible reason can there be for doubting his good faith ?

### THADDEUS.

Thank you.

### ELKIN.

Here is a man who forfeits a considerable sum of money, and deliberately places himself in peril, in order to right a wrong which nobody on earth would have suspected him of committing.  Mr. Mortimore is *accusing* himself of a serious offense, not defending himself from it.

### VALLANCE.

[*Obstinately.*]  What we beg of Mr. Mortimore to do, for the sake of all parties, is to clear up certain inconsistencies in his story with his brothers' account of his movements and  conduct on this Wednesday evening. We are entitled to ask that.

JAMES.

Aye—entitled.

STEPHEN *and* PONTING.

Entitled.

ELKIN.

[*To* JAMES *and* STEPHEN.] Yes, and Mr. Mortimore is equally entitled to refuse it.

JAMES, STEPHEN *and* PONTING.

[*Indignantly.*] Oh —— !

THADDEUS.

But I—I haven't refused.  I—I've done my best ——

ELKIN.

On the other hand, if he has no objection to her doing so, the person to assist you, I suggest—distressing as it may be to her—is the wife.

VALLANCE.

[*Assentingly.*] The wife ——
    [THADDEUS *pushes aside the chair which he is holding and comes to the table.*

ELKIN.

*She* ought to be able to satisfy you as to what time he was with her ——

VALLANCE.

[*To everybody.*] By-the-bye, has she ever mentioned this visit of her husband's to Cannon Row ——?

ANN *and* LOUISA.

Never—never ——

ELKIN.

Attaching no importance to it.  But now——

THADDEUS.

[*Stretching out a quivering hand to them all.*]  No.
No, no.  Don't you—don't you drag my wife into this.
I—I won't have my wife dragged into this——

JAMES.

[*In a blaze.*]  Why not?

STEPHEN.

Why not?

THE LADIES.

[*Indignantly.*]  Ah——!

THADDEUS.

You—you leave my wife out of it——

JAMES.

[*To* THADDEUS, *furiously.*]  Who the hell's your
wife——!

ELKIN *and* VALLANCE.

Gentlemen—gentlemen——

LOUISA.

Who's Phyllis——!

ANN.

Who's *she*——!

ROSE.

Ha!

JAMES *and* STEPHEN.

[*Derisively.*]  Ha, ha, ha!

THADDEUS.

Anyhow, I do object—I do object to your dragging her into it—[*his show of courage flickering away*] I—I do object—[*coming to the nearer side of the table, rather unsteadily*] Mr. Elkin—Mr. Vallance—I—I don't think I can be of any further assistance to you to-day ——

[VALLANCE *shrugs his shoulders at* ELKIN.

ELKIN.

[*To* THADDEUS, *kindly*.] One minute—one minute more. Mr. Vallance has taken down your statement roughly. [*To* VALLANCE.] If you'll read us your notes, Mr. Vallance, Mr. Mortimore will tell us whether they are substantially correct—[*to* THADDEUS] perhaps he will even be willing to attach his name to them ——

[*With a nod of patient acquiescence*, THADDEUS *sinks into the middle chair.* VALLANCE *prepares to read his notes, first making some additions to them.*

JAMES.

[*To* THADDEUS, *from the other side of the table.*] Look here ——!

THADDEUS.

[*Feebly.*] No—no more questions. I—I'm advised I —I may refuse ——

JAMES.

Mr. Vallance asked you just now about your conscience ——

THADDEUS.

I—I'm not going to answer any more questions ——

STEPHEN.

[*To* JAMES.] It was Mr. Elkin ——

JAMES.

I don't care a curse which it was ——

THADDEUS.

No more questions ——

JAMES.

[*Leaning across the table towards* THADDEUS, *fiercely.*]
When the devil did your conscience begin to prick you
over this?  Hey?

STEPHEN.

[*To* THADDEUS.] Yes, you've been in excellent spirits
apparently this last month—excellent spirits.

JAMES.

[*Hammering on the table.*]  Hey?

STEPHEN.

[*To* ELKIN *and* VALLANCE.] There was no sign of
anything amiss when we were with him this afternoon,
gentlemen—none whatever, I give you my word.

JAMES.

Less than two hours ago—not a symptom !

STEPHEN

[*To* JAMES.]  He was gay enough at the club dinner
on Tuesday night.  It was remarked—commented on.

LOUISA.

[*At* STEPHEN'S *elbow, unconsciously.*]  It's Phyllis who's
been ill all the month, not Thaddeus.

JAMES.

[*In the same way, with a hoarse laugh.*]  Ha !  If it had
been his precious wife who'd come to us and told us this
tale ——

STEPHEN.

Yes, if it had been the lady ——

JAMES.

If it had been —— [*Struck by the idea which occurs to him,* JAMES *breaks off.* THADDEUS *doesn't stir.* JAMES, *after a pause, thoughtfully.*] If it had been ——

STEPHEN.

[*Holding his breath, to* JAMES.] Eh?

JAMES.

[*Slowly stroking his beard.*] One might have—understood it ——

ELKIN.

[*Who has been listening attentively, in a tone of polite interest.*] How long has Mrs. Mortimore been indisposed?

JAMES.

[*Disturbed.*] Oh—er—a few weeks ——

VALLANCE.

[*Quietly.*] Ever since —— ?

JAMES.

[*With a nod.*] Aye.
    [ELKIN *and* VALLANCE *look at each other inquiringly.*

STEPHEN.

[*Staring into space.*] Ever since—Edward—as a matter of fact ——

ROSE.

[*Going to* ANN *and* LOUISA.] What's wrong with her? What's wrong with his wife?

*THE  THUNDERBOLT*

ANN.

[*Obtusely.*]  She's not sleeping.


LOUISA.

[*Looking from one to the other.*]  No—she isn't ——
          [*There is a further pause, and then* THADDEUS,
              *slowly turning from the table, rises.*


THADDEUS.

[*In a strange voice, his hands fumbling at the buttons of
his jacket.*]  Well, gentlemen—whatever my sins are—I
—I decline to sit still and hear my wife insulted in this
style.   If it's all the same to you, I'll call round on Mr.
Vallance in the morning and—and sign the paper ——
          [*While* THADDEUS *is speaking,* JAMES *and*
              STEPHEN *come forward on the left,* ELKIN *and*
              VALLANCE *on the right.   The three women get
              together at the back and look on with wide-open
              eyes.   The movement is made gradually and
              noiselessly, so that when* THADDEUS *turns to go
              he is startled at finding his way obstructed.
              After a time* PONTING *also leaves the table,
              watching the proceedings, with a falling jaw,
              from a little distance on the right.*


ELKIN.

[*Rubbing his chin meditatively, to* THADDEUS.]  Mr.
Mortimore, your wife traveled with you and the other
members of the family to Linchpool on the Tuesday ——?


JAMES.

Aye, she was with us ——


ELKIN.

[*To* THADDEUS.]  She was in the railway carriage when
the—when the discussion arose ——?

STEPHEN.

Yes, yes——

ELKIN.

The discussion as to where a man's money goes, in the absence of a will?

ANN.

[*From the other side of the table.*] Yes ——

LOUISA.

[*Close to* ANN.] Of course she was.

ELKIN.

[*Nodding.*] H'm. [*To* THADDEUS.] I—I am most anxious not to pain you unnecessarily. Er—the conversation you had with your brother Edward at the bedside, in reference to Mrs. Thaddeus Mortimore—when he said that he—that he ——

JAMES.

[*Breathing heavily.*] He'd taken a fancy to her ——

ELKIN.

That he wished to make her a present of jewelry—she was within hearing during that talk?

THADDEUS.

[*Avoiding everybody's gaze, his hands twitching involuntarily at his side.*] She—she may have been.

ELKIN.

[*Piercingly.*] He was left in her charge, you know.

THADDEUS.

She—she was moving about the room ——

ELKIN.

She would scarcely have been far away from him.

THADDEUS.
[*Moistening his lips with his tongue.*]  N-no.

ELKIN.
And when he handed you his keys and asked you to
go down-stairs and open the safe—did she hear and wit-
ness that also?

THADDEUS.
She—she—very likely.

ELKIN.
[*Raising his voice.*]  There was nothing at all confi-
dential in this transaction between you and your brother?

THADDEUS.
Why—why should there have been?

ELKIN.
Why *should* there have been?  [*Coming a step nearer
to him.*]  So that, feeling towards her as he did, there
was no reason why, if you hadn't chanced to be on the
spot—there was no reason why he shouldn't have held
that conversation with *her*, and intrusted *her* with the
keys.

THADDEUS.
She—she was almost a stranger to him.  He—he
hadn't seen her since she was a child ——

ELKIN.
[*Interrupting him.*]  Tell us—this illness of Mrs. Mortimore's ——?

THADDEUS.

My—my wife's a nervous, delicate woman—always has been ——

ELKIN.

[*Nodding.*]  Quite so.

THADDEUS.

She—she was upset at being alone with Edward when he—when he swooned ——

JAMES.

That was the tale ——

ELKIN.

[*To* THADDEUS.]  Although you happened to be in the library, a floor or two below, at the time

THADDEUS.

He—he might have died suddenly, in her arms.  She's a nervous, sensitive woman ——

ELKIN.

[*Nodding.*]  And she's been unwell ever since.  [*With an abrupt change of manner.*]  Mr. Mortimore, how is the lock of the safe opened?

THADDEUS.

Opened —— ?

ELKIN.

[*Sharply.*]  The safe in the library in Cannon Row—how do you open it?  [THADDEUS *is silent.*]  Is it a simple lock, or is there anything unusual about it?

THADDEUS.

He—he gave me directions how to open it.

ELKIN.

Tell us ——

THADDEUS.

I—I forget ——

ELKIN.

Forget?

THADDEUS.

It—it's gone from me ——

JAMES.

[*In a low voice.*] Gentlemen, you couldn't forget
*that* ——

STEPHEN.

[*In the same way.*] You *couldn't* forget it

ELKIN.

[*To* THADDEUS, *solemnly.*] Mr. Mortimore, are you
sure that the conversation at the bedside didn't take place
between your brother and your wife solely, and that it
wasn't *she* who was sent down-stairs to fetch the jewelry?

THADDEUS.

[*Drawing himself up, with a last effort.*] Sure ——!

ELKIN.

Are you positive that *she* didn't open the safe?

THADDEUS.

.It—it's ridiculous ——

ELKIN.

[*Quickly.*] When you took her to Roper's, the
draper's, on the Thursday—you left her there?

THADDEUS.

Yes, I—I left her ——

ELKIN.

Are you sure that *she* didn't then go on to the bridge, and tear up the will, and throw the pieces into the river?

THADDEUS.

I—I decline to answer any more questions ——

ELKIN.

[*Raising his voice again.*] Were you in Cannon Row, sir, on the night of June the nineteenth, for a *single moment* between eight o'clock and eleven —— ?

THADDEUS.

[*Losing his head completely.*] Ah! Ah! I know—I know! You mean to drag my wife into this—— !

ELKIN.

[*To* THADDEUS.] You were late in coming here this afternoon, Mr. Mortimore ——

THADDEUS.

[*To* ELKIN, *threateningly.*] Don't you—don't you dare to do it —— !

ELKIN.

Owing, you say, to your having made a communication to Mrs. Mortimore about this affair ——

THADDEUS.

[*Clinging to the chair which is behind him.*] You—you leave my wife out of it —— !

ELKIN.

Are you sure that you were not delayed through having to *receive* a communication from her —— ?

THADDEUS.

[*Dropping into the chair.*] Don't you—drag her—into it——!

ELKIN.

Are you sure that the story you have told us, substituting yourself for the principal person of that story, is not exactly the story which she has just told *you?* [*There is a pause.* PONTING *goes to* ROSE.] Mr. Vallance——

VALLANCE.

Yes?

ELKIN.

I propose to see Mrs. Mortimore in this matter, without delay.

VALLANCE.

Very good.

ELKIN.

Will you——?

VALLANCE.

Certainly.

> [*Quietly,* VALLANCE *returns to the table and, seating himself, again collects his papers.* ELKIN *is following him.*

JAMES.

Mr. Elkin——

ELKIN.

[*Stopping.*] Eh?

JAMES.

Stealing a will—destroying a will—what is it?

ELKIN.

What *is* it?

JAMES.

The law—what's the law ——?

ELKIN.

[*To* JAMES.] I—I'm sorry to have to say, sir—it's a felony.

THADDEUS.

[*With a look of horror.*] Oh ——!

[ANN *and* LOUISA *come to* JAMES *and* STEPHEN *hurriedly.* ELKIN *sits beside* VALLANCE. *and, picking up their bags from the floor, they put away their papers.*

JAMES.

[*Standing over* THADDEUS.] Well! Are yer proud of her now?

STEPHEN.

*This* is what his marriage has ended in!

LOUISA.

I'm not in the least surprised.

ANN.

Old Burdock's daughter!

ROSE.

[*From the other side of the table.*] Thank heaven, my name isn't Mortimore!

THADDEUS.

[*Leaping to his feet in a frenzy.*] Don't you touch her! Don't any of you touch her! Don't you harm a hair of her head! [*To the group on the left.*] You've helped to bring this on her! You've helped to make her life unendurable! You've helped to bring her to this! She's been a good wife to me. Oh, my God, let me get her away! [*Turning towards the door.*] Mr. Elkin—Mr. Vallance—do let me get her away! Don't you harm a hair of her head! Don't you touch her! [*At the door.*] She's been a good wife to me! [*Opening the door and disappearing.*] She's been a good wife to me——!

### JAMES.

[*Moving over to the right, shouting after* THADDEUS.] Been a good wife to you, has she!

### STEPHEN.

[*Also moving to the right.*] A disgrace—a disgrace to the family!

### LOUISA.

[*Following* STEPHEN.] I always said so—I said so till I was tired——

### JAMES.

*We've* helped to bring her to this!

### ANN.

[*Sitting in a chair on the nearer side of the dining-table.*] A vile creature!

### PONTING.

[*Coming forward on the left with* ROSE.] Damn the woman! Damn the woman! My position is a cruel one ——

### STEPHEN.

[*Raising his arms as he paces the room on the right.*] Here's a triumph for Hammond!

JAMES.

[*To* PONTING, *contemptuously.*]  *Your* position —— !

LOUISA.

Nellie Robson's got the better of me now.

PONTING.

[*To* JAMES.]  I'm landed with an enormous house in Carlos Place—my builders are in it ——

ROSE.

[*Pacing the room on the left.*]  Oh, we're in a shocking scrape!   We're up to our necks —— !

JAMES.

[*Approaching* PONTING.]  D'ye think you're the only sufferer —— !

STEPHEN.

[*Wildly.*]  A triumph for Hammond !   A triumph for Hammond !

JAMES.

[*To* PONTING.]  I've bought all that dirt at the bottom of Gordon Street—acres of it —— !

PONTING.

[*Passing him and walking away to the right.*]  That's *your* business.

STEPHEN.

[*Now, with* LOUISA, *at the further side of the dining-table.*]  Hammond and his filthy rag !

JAMES.

[*Going after* PONTING, *in a fury.*]  Aye, it *is* my business ——

PONTING.

[*Turning upon him viciously.*]  I wish to God, sir, **I'd** never seen or heard of you, *or* your family.

ROSE.

[*Coming forward.*]  Oh, Toby, don't ——!

JAMES.

[*To* PONTING.]  You wish that, do yer ——!

ANN.

[*Rising and putting herself between* JAMES *and* PONTING.]  James ——!

STEPHEN.

[*Shaking his fists in the air.*]  Blast Hammond and his filthy rag.

JAMES.

[*To* PONTING.]  You patronizing little pauper ——!

ROSE.

[*To* JAMES.]  Don't you speak to my husband like that ——!

PONTING.

You're a pack of low, common people ——!

ROSE.

[*Going to* PONTING.]  He's the only gentleman among you.

JAMES.

The only gentleman among us ——!

STEPHEN.

[*Coming forward, with* LOUISA, *on the left.*]  The only gentleman ——!

#### JAMES.

We could have done without such a gentleman in our family—[*to* ANN, *who is forcing him, coaxingly, towards the left*] hey, mother?

#### STEPHEN.

[*Advancing to* PONTING, *still followed by* LOUISA.] Exceedingly well—exceedingly well ——

#### LOUISA.

[*Taking* STEPHEN'S *arm.*] Don't lower yourself —— !

#### JAMES.

[*Over* ANN'S *shoulder.*] The Colonel never came near us the other day till he saw a chance o' picking up the pieces ——!

#### STEPHEN.

Nor Rose either—neither of them did !

#### JAMES.

It's six o' one and half a dozen o' the other !

#### ROSE.

[*To* JAMES *and* STEPHEN.] Oh, you cads, you boys —— !

#### JAMES.

[*Mockingly.*] Didn't they bustle down to Linchpool in a hurry *then !* Ha, ha, ha !

#### STEPHEN.

[*Waving his hand in* PONTING'S *face.*] This serves you right, Colonel ; this serves you right.

#### ROSE.

[*Leading* PONTING *towards the door.*] Don't notice them—don't notice them ——

JAMES.

[*Walking about on the left, to* ANN.] I'm in a mess, mother ; I'm in a dreadful mess !

STEPHEN.

[*Sinking into a chair by the tea-table.*] On I go at the broken-down rat-hole in King Street ; on I go with my worn-out old plant ——— !

    [*On getting to the door,* PONTING *discovers that* ELKIN *and* VALLANCE *have taken their departure.  He returns, with* ROSE, *to the further side of the dining-table.*

ANN.

[*To* JAMES.] You must get rid of your contract, James.

JAMES.

Who'll take it—who'll take it ——— !

STEPHEN.

I've always been behind the times ———

LOUISA.

Nelly will laugh her teeth out of her head ———

PONTING.

[*To* JAMES *and* STEPHEN, *trying to attract their attention.*] Mortimore—Mortimore ———

ANN.

[*To* JAMES.] It's splendid land, isn't it ?

JAMES.

Nobody's been ass enough to touch it but me !

STEPHEN.

[*Rocking himself to and fro.*] Always behind the times —no need to tell me that ———

PONTING.

[*To* JAMES.] Mortimore ——

JAMES.

[*To* PONTING.] What?

PONTING.

[*Pointing to the empty chairs.*] They've gone ——

JAMES.

[*Sobering down.*] Hooked it ——

STEPHEN.

[*Looking round.*] Gone —— ?

JAMES.

Elkin ——

STEPHEN.

[*Weakly.*] And Vallance ——

JAMES.

They might have had the common civility ——

PONTING.

[*Coming forward slowly and dejectedly.*] They've gone to that woman ——

ROSE.

[*At the further side of the table.*] I hope they send her to jail—the trull—the baggage —— !

[ANN *and* LOUISA *join* ROSE.

PONTING.

The whole business will be settled between 'em in ten minutes—the whole business ——

JAMES.

[*Coming to* PONTING.]  Aye, the whole concern.

STEPHEN.

[*Who has risen, holding his head.*]  Oh, it's awful!

PONTING.

[*Laying a hand on* JAMES *and* STEPHEN *who are on either side of him.*]  My friends, don't let us disagree—we're all in the same boat——

JAMES.

[*Grimly, looking into space.*]  Aye, they'll be talking it over nicely ——

PONTING.

Let us stick to each other.   Aren't we throwing up the sponge prematurely —— ?

JAMES.

[*Not heeding him.*]  Tad and his wife and the lawyers —ha, ha —— !

STEPHEN.

And that girl ——

JAMES.

[*Nodding.*]  The young lady.

PONTING.

What girl?

STEPHEN.

Miss Thornhill.

PONTING.

Thornhill —— ?

JAMES.

She's staying with 'em.

PONTING.

*She* is !

ROSE.

[*Coming forward on the left.*] Staying with the Tads ——?

PONTING.

In their house ! Elkin and Vallance will find her there !

JAMES.

[*Nodding.*] Aye.

PONTING.

[*Violently.*] It's a conspiracy ——?

JAMES.

Conspiracy ——?

PONTING.

I see it ! The Thornhill girl's in it ! She's at the bottom of it ! [*Going to* ROSE *as* ANN *and* LOUISA *come forward on the left.*] They're cheating us—they're cheating us. I tell you we ought to be present. They're robbing us behind our backs ——

STEPHEN.

[*Looking at* JAMES.] Jim ——?

JAMES.

[*Shaking his head.*] No, it's no conspiracy ——

PONTING.

It is ! They're robbing us ——!

STEPHEN.

[*To* JAMES.]  Still, I—I really think ——

PONTING.

Behind our backs !

THE LADIES.

Yes—yes—yes ——

JAMES.

[*After a pause, quietly, stroking his beard.*]  By George, we'll go down ——— !

[*Instantly they all make for the door.*

STEPHEN.

We'll be there as soon as Elkin ——

PONTING.

A foul conspiracy ——— !

ANN.

[*In the rear.*]  Wait till I put on my hat——

ROSE.

Jim, you follow with Ann.

PONTING.

[*To* STEPHEN.]  We'll go on ahead.

STEPHEN.

Yes, we'll go first.

LOUISA.

I'm ready.

JAMES.

No, no ; we'll all go together.

PONTING.

Robbing us behind our backs ——— !

JAMES.

Look sharp, mother !

THE OTHERS.

Be quick—be quick—be quick ——— !
[*Seizing* ANN *and pushing her before them, they struggle through the doorway.*

### END OF THE THIRD ACT

# THE FOURTH ACT

*The scene is the same, in every respect, as that of the Second Act.*

VALLANCE *is seated at the writing-table by the bay-window, reading aloud from a written paper.* PHYLLIS, *in deep abasement, is upon the settee by the piano, and* THADDEUS *is standing by her, holding her left hand in both of his. On the left of the table at the end of the piano sits* HELEN, *pale, calm, and erect, and opposite to her, in the chair on the other side of the table, is* ELKIN. PONTING *is sitting in the bay-window,* STEPHEN *is standing upon the hearth-rug, and the rest of the "family" are seated about the room—all looking very humble and downcast.* ANN *and* LOUISA *are upon the settee on the right,* ROSE *is in the armchair on the nearer side of the fireplace,* JAMES *on the ottoman.* ROSE, ANN, *and* LOUISA *are in their outdoor things.*

### VALLANCE.

[*Reading.*] "It was broad daylight before my husband and I got back to our lodgings. The document was then in a pocket I was wearing under my dress. Before going to bed I hid the pocket in a drawer. At about eleven o'clock on the same morning my husband took me to Roper's, the draper's, in Ford Street, and left me there. After my measurements were taken I went up Ford Street and on to the bridge. I then tore up both the paper and the envelope and dropped the pieces into the water."

202

ELKIN.

[*Half turning to* PHYLLIS.] You declare that that is correct in every particular, Mrs. Mortimore?

[PHYLLIS *bursts into a paroxysm of tears.*

THADDEUS.

[*To* PHYLLIS, *as if comforting a child.*] All right, dear; all right. I'm with you—I'm with you. [*She sobs helplessly.*] Tell Mr. Elkin—tell him—is that correct?

PHYLLIS.

[*Through her sobs.*] Yes.

ELKIN.

[*To* PHYLLIS.] You've nothing further to say?

[*Her sobbing continues.*

THADDEUS.

[*To* PHYLLIS.] Have you anything more to say, dear? [*Encouragingly, as she tries to speak.*] I'm here, dear— I'm with you. Is there anything—anything more——?

PHYLLIS.

Only—only that I beg Miss Thornhill's pardon. I beg her pardon. Oh, I beg her pardon.

[ELKIN *looks at* HELEN, *who, however, makes no response.*

THADDEUS.

[*To* PHYLLIS, *glancing at the others.*] And—and ——

PHYLLIS.

And—and Ann and Jim—and Stephen—and Lou—and Rose and Colonel Ponting—I beg their pardon—I beg their pardon.

[*She sinks back upon the settee, and her fit of weeping gradually exhausts itself.*

THADDEUS.

And I—and I, Mr. Elkin—I wish to offer *my* apologies
—my humble apologies—to you and Mr. Vallance—and
to everybody—for what took place this afternoon in my
brother's dining-room.

ELKIN.

[*Kindly.*]  Perhaps it isn't necessary ——

THADDEUS.

Perhaps not—but it's on my mind.  [*To* ELKIN *and*
VALLANCE.]  I assure you and Mr. Vallance—[*to the
others*] and I assure every member of my family—that
when I went away from here I had no intention of invent-
ing the story I attempted to tell you at "Ivanhoe."   It
came into my head suddenly—quite suddenly—on my
way to Claybrook Road—almost at the gate of the house.
I must have been mad to think I could succeed in impos-
ing on you all.   I believe I *was* mad, gentlemen ; and
that's my excuse, and I—I hope you'll accept it.

ELKIN.

Speaking for myself, I accept it freely.

VALLANCE.

And I.

THADDEUS.

Thank you—thank you.
        [*He looks at the others wistfully, but they are all
            staring at the carpet, and they, too, make no
            response.   Then he seats himself beside* PHYLLIS
            *and again takes her hand.*

ELKIN.

[*After a pause.*]  Well, Mr. Vallance ——  [VALLANCE
*rises, the written paper in his hand, and comes forward*

*on the left.*] I think—[*glancing over his shoulder at*
PHYLLIS] I think that this lady makes it perfectly clear
to any reasonable person that the document which she
abstracted from the safe in Cannon Row, and subse-
quently destroyed, was the late Mr. Edward Mortimore's
will, and that Miss Thornhill was the universal legatee
under it, and was named as the sole executrix. [VAL-
LANCE *seats himself in the chair on the extreme left.*] As
I said in Mr. James Mortimore's house, the advice I shall
give to Miss Thornhill is that she applies to the Court for
probate of the substance and effect of this will.

### VALLANCE.

Upon an affidavit by Mrs. Thaddeus Mortimore ——?

### ELKIN.

An affidavit disclosing what she has done and verifying
a statement of the contents of the will.

### VALLANCE.

And how, may I ask, are you going to get over your
great difficulty ?

### ELKIN.

My great difficulty ——?

### VALLANCE.

The fact that Mrs. Thaddeus Mortimore is unable to
swear that the will was duly witnessed.

### PONTING.

Ah ! [*Rising and coming forward, but discreetly keeping behind* HELEN.] That seems to me to be insuperable
—insuperable. [*Anxiously.*] Eh, Mr. Vallance?

### STEPHEN.

[*Advancing a step or two.*] An obstacle which cannot
be got over.

### PONTING.

[*Eyeing* HELEN *furtively.*] It—ah—may appear rather ungracious to Miss Thornhill—a young lady we hold in the highest esteem—and to whom I express regret for any hasty word I may have used on arriving here—unreserved regret—[HELEN'S *eyes flash, and her shoulders contract ; otherwise she makes no acknowledgment*] it may appear ungracious to Miss Thornhill to discuss this point in her presence ; [*pulling at his moustache*] but she will be the first to recognize that there are many—ah—interests at stake.

### STEPHEN.

Many interests—many interests ——

### PONTING.

And where so many interests are involved, one mustn't —ah—allow oneself to be swayed by anything like sentiment.

### STEPHEN.

[*At the round table.*] In justice, one *oughtn't* to be sentimental.

### PONTING.

One *daren't* be sentimental.

### LOUISA.

[*Meekly, raising her head.*] I always maintain ——

### STEPHEN.

[*To* LOUISA.] Yes, yes, yes.

### LOUISA.

There are two sides ——

STEPHEN.

Yes, yes.

ELKIN.

[*Ignoring the interruption.*] Mrs. Thaddeus Mortimore is prepared to swear, Mr. Vallance, that she believes there were other signatures besides the signature of the late Mr. Mortimore.

VALLANCE.

But she has no recollection of the names of witnesses——

PONTING.

None whatever.

STEPHEN.

Not the faintest.

VALLANCE.

Nor as to whether there was an attestation clause at all.

PONTING.

Her memory is an utter blank as to that.

STEPHEN.

An utter blank.
[*As* PONTING *and* STEPHEN *perk up, there is a rise in the spirits of the ladies at the fireplace.* ROSE *twists her chair round to face the men.* JAMES *doesn't stir.*

ELKIN.

Notwithstanding that, I can't help considering it reasonably probable that, in the circumstances, the Court would presume the will to have been made in due form.

PONTING.
[*Walking about agitatedly.*]  I differ.

STEPHEN.
[*Walking about.*]  So do I.

PONTING.
I don't pretend to a profound knowledge of the law ——

STEPHEN.
As a mere layman, *I* consider it extremely *im*probable —extremely *im*probable.

VALLANCE.
[*To* STEPHEN *and* PONTING.]  Well, gentlemen, there I am inclined to agree with you ——

PONTING.
[*Pulling himself up.*]  Ah !

STEPHEN.
[*Returning to the round table.*]  Ah !

VALLANCE.
*I* think it doubtful whether, on the evidence of Mrs. Thaddeus Mortimore, the will could be upheld.

PONTING.
Exactly.  [*To everybody.*]  You've only to look at the thing in the light of common sense ——

STEPHEN.
[*Argumentatively, rapping the table.*]  A will exists or it does not exist ——

PONTING.
If it ever existed, and has been destroyed ——

STEPHEN.

It must be shown that it was a complete will——

PONTING.

Shown beyond dispute.

STEPHEN.

Complete down to the smallest detail.

VALLANCE.

[*Continuing.*] At the same time, in my opinion, the facts do not warrant the making of an affidavit that the late Mr. Mortimore died intestate.

PONTING.

[*Stiffly.*] Indeed?

STEPHEN.

[*Depressed.*] Really?

VALLANCE.

And the question of whether or not he left a duly executed will is clearly one for the Court to decide.

ELKIN.

Quite so—quite so.

VALLANCE.

I advise, therefore, that, to get the question determined, the next-of-kin should consent to the course of procedure suggested by Mr. Elkin.

ELKIN.

I am assuming their consent.

PONTING.

[*Blustering.*] And supposing the next-of-kin do *not* consent, Mr. Vallance ——?

STEPHEN.

Supposing we do *not* consent —— ?

PONTING.

Supposing we are convinced—convinced—that the late Mr. Mortimore died without leaving a properly executed will?

ELKIN.

Then the application, instead of being by motion to the judge in Court, must take the form of an action by writ. [*To* VALLANCE.] In any case, perhaps it should do so.

> [*There is a pause.* STEPHEN *wanders disconsolately to the window on the right and stands gazing into the garden.* PONTING *leans his elbows on the piano and stares at vacancy.*

ELKIN.

[*To* HELEN, *looking at his watch.*] Well, my dear Miss Thornhill —— ?

> [VALLANCE *rises.*

HELEN.

Wait—wait a moment ——

> [*The sound of* HELEN'S *voice turns everybody, except* JAMES, THADDEUS, *and* PHYLLIS, *in her direction.*

ELKIN.

[*To* HELEN.] Eh ?

HELEN.

Wait a moment, please. There is something I want to be told—there's something I want to be told plainly.

ELKIN.

What ?

HELEN.

Mrs. Thaddeus Mortimore ——

ELKIN.

Yes?

HELEN.

[*Slowly.*] I want to know whether it is necessary, what-ever proceedings are taken on my behalf—whether it is necessary that she should be publicly disgraced. I want to know that.

ELKIN.

Whichever course is adopted—motion to the judge or action by writ—Mrs. Thaddeus Mortimore's act must be disclosed in open Court.

HELEN.

There are no means of avoiding it?

ELKIN.

None.

HELEN.

And the offence she has committed is—felony, you say?

     [ELKIN *inclines his head. Again there is silence,*
         *during which* HELEN *sits with knitted brows,*
         *and then* JAMES *rouses himself and looks up.*

JAMES.

[ *To* ELKIN.] What's the—what's the penalty?

ELKIN.

[*Turning to him.*] The—the penalty?

JAMES.

The legal punishment.

ELKIN.

I think—another occasion ——
> [*Suddenly* THADDEUS *and* PHYLLIS *rise together,*
> *he with an arm round her, supporting her,*
> *and they stand side by side like criminals in the*
> *dock.*

THADDEUS.

[*Quickly.*]  No, no—now ——

PHYLLIS.

[*Faintly.*]  Yes—now ——

THADDEUS.

[*To* ELKIN *and* VALLANCE.]  We—we should like to know the worst, gentlemen.   I—I had the idea from the first that it was a serious offence—but hardly so serious ——

ELKIN.

[*With a wave of the hand.*]  By and by ——

THADDEUS.

Oh, you needn't hesitate, Mr. Elkin.  [*Drawing* PHYLLIS *closer to him.*]  We—we shall go through with it.   We shall go through with it to the end.  [*A pause.*]  Imprisonment, sir?

ELKIN.

[*Gravely.*]  A person convicted of stealing or destroying a will for a fraudulent purpose is liable under the statute to varying terms of penal servitude, or to imprisonment with or without hard labor.   In this instance, we should be justified, I am sure, in hoping for a considerable amount of leniency.
> [THADDEUS *and* PHYLLIS *slowly look at one an-*
> *other with expressionless faces.*  JAMES *rises*
> *and moves away to the fireplace where he*

*stands looking down upon the flowers in the
grate.* VALLANCE *goes to the writing-table
and puts the written paper into his bag.* ELKIN
*rises, takes up his bag from the table at the
end of the piano, and is following* VALLANCE.
*As he passes* HELEN, *she lays her hand upon
his arm.*

HELEN.

Mr. Elkin ——

ELKIN.

[*Stopping.*] Yes?

HELEN.

Oh, but this is impossible.

ELKIN.

Impossible?

HELEN.

Quite impossible.  I couldn't be a party—please understand me—I refuse to be a party—to any steps which
would bring ruin on Mrs. Mortimore.

ELKIN.

[*Politely.*] You refuse —— ?

HELEN.

Absolutely.  At any cost—at any cost to me—we must
all unite in sparing her and her husband and children.

ELKIN.

My dear young lady, I join you heartily in your desire
not to bring suffering upon innocent people.  But if you
decline to take proceedings——

HELEN.

There is no "if" in the matter——

ELKIN.

If you decline to take proceedings, there is a deadlock.

HELEN.

A deadlock?

ELKIN.

As Mr. Vallance tells us, it's out of the question that the next-of-kin should now apply for Letters of Administration in the usual way.

HELEN.

Why? I don't see why—I can't see why.

ELKIN.

[*Pointing to* JAMES *and* STEPHEN.] You don't see why neither of these gentlemen can make an affidavit that Mr. Edward Mortimore died intestate!

HELEN.

[*With a movement of the head towards* PHYLLIS.] She has no remembrance of a—what is it called ——?

PONTING.

[*Eagerly.*] Attestation clause.

STEPHEN.

[*Coming to the head of the piano.*] Attestation clause.

HELEN.

[*Haughtily, without turning.*] Thank you. [*To* ELKIN.] Only the vaguest notion that there *were* witnesses.

PONTING.

The vaguest notion.

STEPHEN.

The haziest.

ELKIN.

Her memory is uncertain there. [*To* HELEN.] But you know—*you know*, Miss Thornhill—as we all know—that it was your father's will that was found in the safe at Cannon Row and destroyed.

HELEN.

[*Looking up at him, gripping the arms of her chair.*] Yes, of course I know it. Thank God I know it! I'm happy in knowing it. I know he didn't forget me ; I know I was all to him that I imagined myself to be. And it's because I've come to know this at last—through *her* —that I can afford to be a little generous to her. Oh, please don't think that I want to introduce sentimentality into this affair—[*with a contemptuous glance at* PONTING *and* STEPHEN] any more than Colonel Ponting does—or Mr. Stephen Mortimore. Mrs. Thaddeus did a cruel thing when she destroyed that will. It's no excuse for her to say that she wasn't aware of my existence. She was defrauding *some* woman ; and, as it happened—I own it now !—defrauding that woman, not only of money, but of what is more valuable than money—of peace of mind, contentment, belief in one who could never speak, never explain, never defend himself. However, she has made the best reparation it is in her power to make—and she has gone through a bad time—and I forgive her. [PHYLLIS *releases herself from* THADDEUS *and drops down upon the settee. He sits upon the ottoman, burying his face in his hands.* HELEN *rises, struggling to keep back her tears, and turns to the door.*] I—I'll go up-stairs—if you'll allow me ——

ELKIN.

[*Between her and the door.*] Miss Thornhill, **you put** us in a position of great difficulty ——

HELEN.

[*Impatiently.*] I say again, I don't see why. Where is the difficulty? [*To* VALLANCE *and* ELKIN.] If there's a difficulty, it's you gentlemen who are raising it. Let the affair go on as it was going on. [*Turning to* JAMES.] Mr. Mortimore! [*To* ELKIN.] I say, let Mr. James Mortimore and the others administer the estate as they intended to do. [*To* JAMES, *who has left the fireplace and slowly advanced to her.*] Mr. Mortimore ——

ELKIN.

[*To* HELEN.] Then you would have Mr. James Mortimore deliberately swear that he believes his late brother died without leaving a will?

HELEN.

Certainly, if necessary. Who would be hurt by it?

ELKIN.

[*Pursing his lips.*] Miss Thornhill——

HELEN.

[*Hotly.*] Why, which do you think would be the more acceptable to the Almighty—that I should send this poor lady to prison, or that Mr. James should take a false oath?

ELKIN.

H'm! I won't attempt to follow you quite so far. But even then a most important point would remain to be settled.

HELEN.

Even then ——?

ELKIN.

Assuming that Mr. James Mortimore did make this affidavit—that he were permitted to make such an affidavit ——

HELEN.

Yes?

ELKIN.

What about the disposition of the estate?

HELEN.

[*Nodding, slowly and thoughtfully.*] The—the disposition of the estate——

> [STEPHEN *steals over to* PONTING, *and* ROSE, ANN, *and* LOUISA *quietly rise and gather together. They all listen with painful interest.*]

ELKIN.

[*To* HELEN.] Morally, at all events, the whole of the late Mr. Mortimore's estate belongs to you.

HELEN.

[*Simply.*] It was his intention that it should do so. [*Looking at* JAMES, *as if inviting him to speak.*] Well——?

JAMES.

[*Stroking his beard.*] Look here, Miss Thornhill. [*Pointing to the chair on the extreme left.*] Sit down a minute. [*She sits.* JAMES *also seats himself, facing her, at the right of the table at the end of the piano.* VALLANCE *joins* ELKIN *and they stand near* HELEN, *occasionally exchanging remarks with each other.*] Look here. [*In a deep, gruff voice.*] There *is* no doubt that my brother Ned's money rightfully belongs to you.

PONTING.

[*Nervously.*] Mortimore ——

JAMES.

[*Turning upon him.*] You leave us alone. Don't you interfere. [*To* HELEN.] I've no more doubt about it, Miss

Thornhill, than that I'm sitting here. Very good. Say
I make the affidavit, and that we—the family—obtain
Letters of Administration. What then? The money
comes to *us*. Still—it's *yours*. We get hold of it, but
it's *yours*. Now! What if we offer to throw the whole
lot, so to speak, into your lap?

#### STEPHEN.

[*Biting his nails.*] Jim ——

#### JAMES.

[*To* STEPHEN.] Don't you interfere. [*To* HELEN.]
I repeat, what if we offer to throw the whole lot into your
lap? [*Leaning forward, very earnestly.*] Miss Thornhill——

#### PONTING.

May I ——?

#### JAMES.

[*To* PONTING.] If you can't be silent——! [*To*
HELEN.] Miss Thornhill, we're poor, we Mortimores.
I won't say anything about Rose—[*with a sneer*] it
wouldn't be polite to the Colonel ; nor Tad—you see
what he's come to. But Stephen and me—take our case.
[*To* ELKIN *and* VALLANCE.] Mr. Vallance—Mr. Elkin
—this is sacred. [*To* HELEN.] My dear, we're promi-
nent men in the town, both of us ; we're looked up to as
being fairly warm and comfortable ; but in reality we're
not much better off than the others. My trade's being
cut into on all sides ; Stephen's business has run to seed ;
we've no capital ; we've never had any capital. What
we might have saved has been spent on educating our
children, and keeping up appearances ; and when the
time comes for us to be knocked out, there'll be precious
little—bar a stroke of luck—precious little for us to end
our days on. So this is a terrible disappointment to us—

an awful disappointment. Aye, the money's yours—it's yours—but—[*opening his hands*] what are you going to do for the family?

> [*There is a pause.  The* PONTINGS, STEPHEN, ANN *and* LOUISA *draw a little nearer*.

#### HELEN.

[*To* JAMES.] Well—since you put it in this way—I'll tell you what I'll do. [*Another pause.*] I'll share with you all.

#### JAMES.

[*To the others.*] You leave us alone ; you leave us alone. [*To* HELEN.] Share and share alike?

#### HELEN.

[*Thinking.*] Share and share alike—after discharging my obligations.

#### JAMES.

Obligations?

#### PONTING *and* STEPHEN.

Obligations?

#### HELEN.

After carrying out my father's instructions with regard to his old servants.

#### JAMES.

[*Nodding.*] Oh, aye.

#### PONTING.

[*Walking about excitedly.*] That's a small matter.

#### STEPHEN.

[*Also walking about.*] A trifle—a trifle ——

PONTING.

Then what it amounts to is this—the estate will be divided into five parts instead of four.

STEPHEN.

Five instead of four—obviously.

HELEN.

[*Still thinking.*] No—into six.

JAMES.

Six?

PONTING *and* STEPHEN.

Six!

ROSE *and* LOUISA.

[*Who with* ANN, *are moving round the head of the piano, to join* PONTING *and* STEPHEN.] Six!

HELEN.

[*Firmly.*] Six. A share must be given, as a memorial of my father, to one of the hospitals in Linchpool.

PONTING *and* STEPHEN.

[*Protestingly.*] Oh ——!

ROSE, ANN *and* LOUISA.

Oh ——!

PONTING.

Entirely unnecessary.

STEPHEN.

Uncalled for.

HELEN.

I insist.

PONTING.

[*Coming to* HELEN.] My dear Miss Thornhill, believe me—believe me—these cadging hospitals are a great deal too well off as it is.

HELEN.

I insist that a share shall be given to a Linchpool hospital.

PONTING.

I could furnish you with details of maladministration on the part of hospital-boards ——

ROSE.

Shocking mismanagement ——

STEPHEN.

There's our own hospital ——

LOUISA.

A scandal.

STEPHEN.

Our Jubilee hospital ——

ANN.

It's scarcely fit to send your servants to.

HELEN.

[*To* JAMES, *rising.*] Mr. Mortimore ——

JAMES.

[*Rising, to* PONTING *and the rest.*] Miss Thornhill says that one share of the estate's to go to a Linchpool hospital. D'ye hear? [*Moving towards them authoritatively.*] That's enough.

[PONTING *and* STEPHEN *bustle to the writing-table, where they each seize a sheet of paper and proceed to reckon.* ROSE, ANN *and* LOUISA *surround them.* JAMES *stands by, his hands in his pockets, looking on.*

PONTING.

[*Sitting at the writing-table—in an undertone.*] A hundred and seventy thousand pounds ——

STEPHEN.

[*Bending over the table—in an undertone.*] Six into seventeen—two and carry five ——

PONTING.

Six into fifty—eight and carry two ——

STEPHEN.

Six into twenty ——

PONTING.

Three ——

[HELEN *seats herself in the chair on the right of the table at the end of the piano.* ELKIN *and* VALLANCE *are now in earnest conversation on the extreme left. While the calculation is going on,* THADDEUS *and* PHYLLIS *raise their heads and look at each other.*

STEPHEN.

Carry two ——

PONTING.

Six into twenty again—three and carry two ——

STEPHEN.

Again, six into twenty—three and carry two ——

PONTING.

Six into forty—six and carry four——

STEPHEN.

Six into forty-eight ——

PONTING.

Eight——

STEPHEN.

Twenty-eight thousand, three hundred and thirty-three pounds, six shillings and eight pence.

PONTING.

[*Rising, his paper in his hand.*] Twenty-eight thousand apiece.

THADDEUS.

[*Rising.*] No ——

PHYLLIS.

[*Rising.*] No ——

THADDEUS.

[*As everybody turns to him.*] No, no —

JAMES.

Eh ?

PONTING.

[*To* THADDEUS.] What do you mean, sir?

STEPHEN.

[*To* THADDEUS.] What do you mean ?

THADDEUS.

[*Agitatedly.*] I don't take my share—my wife and I don't take our share—we don't touch it ——

PHYLLIS.

[*Clinging to* THADDEUS.] We won't touch it—oh, **no**, no, no, no —— !

JAMES.

[*To* THADDEUS.] Don't be a fool—don't be a fool!

THADDEUS.

Fool or no fool—not a penny ——

PHYLLIS.

Not a penny of it ——

THADDEUS.

Not a penny.

HELEN.

Very well, then. [*In a clear voice.*] Very well; **Mr.** Thaddeus Mortimore will not accept his share.

PONTING.

[*With alacrity.*] He declines it.

HELEN.

He declines it.

PONTING.

That alters the figures—alters the figures ——

STEPHEN.

Very materially.

ROSE.

[*To* ANN *and* LOUISA.] Only five to share instead of six.

ANN.

[*Bewildered.*] I don't understand ——

LOUISA.

[*Shaking her arm.*] Five instead of six!
[*Laying his paper on the top of the piano,* PONTING
*produces his pocket-pencil and makes a fresh
calculation.* STEPHEN *stands at his elbow.*
ROSE, ANN *and* LOUISA *gather round them.*

STEPHEN.

[*In an undertone.*] A hundred and seventy thousand ——

PONTING.

[*In an undertone.*] *Five* into seventeen ——

STEPHEN.

Three ——

PONTING.

Five into twenty ——

STEPHEN.

Thirty-four thousand exactly.

PONTING.

Thirty-four thousand apiece.

ROSE, ANN *and* LOUISA.

[*To each other.*] Thirty-four thousand!

HELEN.

Wait—wait. Wait, please. [*After a short pause.*] Mr.
Thaddeus Mortimore refuses to accept his share. I am
sorry—but he appears determined.

THADDEUS.

Determined—determined ——

### PHYLLIS.

Determined ——

### HELEN.

That being so, I ask that his share shall be settled upon his boy and girl. [*To* ELKIN.] Mr. Elkin —— [ELKIN *advances to her.*] I suppose an arrangement of that kind can easily be made?

### ELKIN.

[*With a shrug.*] Mr. Thaddeus Mortimore can assent to his share being handed over to the trustees of a Deed of Settlement for the benefit of his children, giving a release to the administrator from all claims in respect of his share.

### HELEN.

[*Turning to* THADDEUS.] You've no objection to this? [THADDEUS *and* PHYLLIS *stare at* HELEN *dumbly, with parted lips.*] They are great friends of mine—Cyril and Joyce—and I hope they'll remain so. [*A pause.*] Well? You've no right to stand in their light. [*A pause.*] You won't, surely, stand in their light? [*A pause.*] Don't.

> [*Again there is silence, and then* PHYLLIS, *leaving* THADDEUS, *totters forward, and drops on her knees before* HELEN, *bowing her head in* HELEN'S *lap.*

### PHYLLIS.

[*Weeping.*] Oh-oh-oh —— !

> [*Calmly,* HELEN *disengages herself from* PHYLLIS, *rises, and walks away to the fireplace.* THADDEUS *lifts* PHYLLIS *from the ground and leads her to the open window. They stand there, facing the garden, she crying upon his shoulder.*

ELKIN.

[*Advancing to the middle of the room, with the air of a man who is about to perform an unpleasant task.*] Miss Thornhill—[HELEN *turns to him*] Mr. Vallance and I— [*to* VALLANCE] Mr. Vallance—[VALLANCE *advances*] Mr. Vallance and I have come to the conclusion that, as all persons interested in this business are *sui juris* and agreeable to the compromise which has been proposed, nobody would be injured by the next-of-kin applying for Letters of Administration.

VALLANCE.

[*To* ELKIN.] Except the Revenue.

ELKIN.

[*Indifferently, with a nod.*] The Revenue.

VALLANCE.

The legacy duty being at three per cent. instead of ten.

ELKIN.

[*Nodding.*] H'm, h'm! [*To* HELEN.] But, my dear young lady, we have also to say that, with the information we possess, we do not see our way clear to act in the matter any further.

VALLANCE.

[*To* JAMES, *who has come forward on the left.*] We certainly could not be parties to the making of an affidavit that the deceased died intestate.

ELKIN.

We couldn't reconcile ourselves to *that*.

VALLANCE.

We leave it, therefore, to the next-of-kin to take their own course for obtaining Letters of Administration.

ELKIN.

In fact, we beg to be allowed to withdraw from the affair altogether.  I speak for myself, at any rate.

VALLANCE.

[*Emphatically.*]  Altogether.

JAMES.

[*After a pause.*]  Oh—all right, Mr. Elkin ; all right, Mr. Vallance.

HELEN.

[*To* ELKIN.]  Then—do I lose you ——?

ELKIN.

I am afraid—for the present ——

HELEN.

[*With dignity.*]  As you please.  I am very grateful to you for what you *have* done for me.

ELKIN.

[*Looking round.*]  If I may offer a last word of advice, it is that you should avoid putting the terms of this compromise into writing.

VALLANCE.

[*Assentingly.*]  Each party must rely upon the other to fulfil the terms honorably.

ELKIN.

[*To* HELEN.]  You have no *legal* right to enforce those terms ; but pray remember that, in the event of any breach of faith, there would be nothing to prevent you propounding the will even after Letters of Administration have been granted.

JAMES.

Breach of faith, sir —— !

PONTING *and* STEPHEN.

[*Indignantly.*] Oh —— !

JAMES.

There's no need, Mr. Elkin ——

ELKIN.

[*To* JAMES.] No, no, no—not the slightest, I'm convinced. [*To* HELEN, *taking her hand.*] The little hotel in London—Norfolk Street —— ?

HELEN.

Till I'm suited with lodgings.

ELKIN.

Mrs. Elkin will write.

HELEN.

My love to her.
  [*He smiles at her and leaves her, as* VALLANCE
    *comes to her and shakes her hand.*

VALLANCE.

[*To* HELEN.] Good-bye.

HELEN.

[*To* VALLANCE.] Good-bye.

ELKIN.

[*To those on the left.*] Good-afternoon.

A MURMUR.

Good-afternoon.

VALLANCE.

[*To those on the left.*]  Good-afternoon.

A MURMUR.

Good-afternoon.
> [JAMES *has opened the door.*  ELKIN *and* VAL-
> LANCE, *carrying their bags, go out.*  JAMES
> *follows them, closing the door.*

PONTING.

[*Coming forward.*]  Ha !  We can replace *those* gentlemen without much difficulty.

STEPHEN.

[*Coming forward.*]  Old  Crake  has gone to pieces and
this fellow Vallance is playing ducks and drakes with the
practice—ducks and drakes.

PONTING.

[*Offering his hand to* HELEN, *who takes it perfunctorily.*]
Greatly  indebted  to  you—greatly  indebted  to  you  for
meeting us half-way and saving unpleasantness.

STEPHEN.

Pratt is the best lawyer in the town—the best by far.

PONTING.

[*To* HELEN.]  Nothing  like a compromise, provided it
can be arrived at—ah ——

STEPHEN.

Without loss of self-respect on both sides.
> [JAMES *returns*.

PONTING.

[*To* JAMES.]  Mortimore, we'll go back to your house.
There are two or three things to talk over ——
> [ROSE *comes to* HELEN *as* PONTING *goes to*
> STEPHEN *and* JAMES.

#### ROSE.

[*Shaking hands with* HELEN.] We sha'n't be settled in Carlos Place till the autumn, but directly we *are* settled ——

#### HELEN.

[*Distantly.*] Thank you.

#### ROSE.

Everybody flocks to my Tuesdays. Let me have your address and I'll send you a card.

[ROSE *leaves* HELEN, *making way for* LOUISA *and* STEPHEN.

#### LOUISA.

[*To* HELEN.] Don't forget the Crescent. Whenever you want to visit your dear father's birthplace ——

#### STEPHEN.

[*Benevolently.*] And if there should be any little ceremony over laying the foundation-stone of the new *Times and Mirror* building ——

#### LOUISA.

There's the spare bedroom.

[*They shake hands with her and, making way for* ANN *and* JAMES, *follow the* PONTINGS, *who have gone out.*

#### ANN.

[*Shaking hands with* HELEN, *gloomily.*] The next time you stay at "Ivanhoe," I hope you'll unpack more than one small trunk. But, there—[*kissing her*] I bear no malice.

[*She follows the others, leaving* JAMES *with* HELEN.

#### JAMES.

[*To* HELEN, *gruffly, wringing her hand.*] Much obliged to you, my dear ; much obliged to you.

HELEN.

[*After glancing over her shoulder, in a whisper.*] Mr.
Mortimore ——

JAMES.

Eh?

HELEN.

[*With a motion of her head in the direction of* THAD-
DEUS *and* PHYLLIS.] These two—these two ——

JAMES.
[*Lowering his voice.*] What about 'em?

HELEN.

She's done a wrong thing, but recollect—you all profit
by it. You don't disdain, any of you, to profit by it.
[*He looks at her queerly, but straight in the eyes.*] Try to
make their lives a little easier for them.

JAMES.

Easier —— ?

HELEN.

Happier. You can influence the others, if you will.
[*A pause.*] Will you?
　　　　[*He reflects, shakes her hand again, and goes to
　　　　the door.*

JAMES.

[*At the door, sharply.*] Tad ——! [THADDEUS *turns.*]
See you in the morning. Phyllis ——! [*She also turns
to him, half scared at his tone.*] See you both in the
morning. [*Nodding to her.*] Good-bye, old girl.
　　　　[*He disappears.* HELEN *is now standing upon
　　　　the hearth-rug, her hands behind her, looking
　　　　down into the grate.* THADDEUS *and* PHYLLIS
　　　　glance at her; then, guiltily, they too move to
　　　　the door, passing round the head of the piano.*

PHYLLIS.

[*At the door in a low, hard voice.*] Helen —— [HELEN *partly turns.*] You're leaving to-morrow. I'll keep out of your way—I'll keep up-stairs in my room—till you've gone.

[*She goes out.* THADDEUS *is following her, when* HELEN *calls to him.*

HELEN.

Mr. Thaddeus —— [*He closes the door and advances to her humbly. She comes forward.*] There's no reason why I should put your wife to that trouble. It's equally convenient to me to return to London this evening. [*He bows.*] Will you kindly ask Kate to pack me?

THADDEUS.

Certainly.

HELEN.

Er—[*thinking*] Mr. Trist had some calls to make after we left the flower-show. If I've gone before he comes back, tell him I'll write ——

THADDEUS.

[*Bowing again.*] You'll write.

HELEN.

And explain.

THADDEUS.

[*Under his breath, looking up quickly.*] Explain ——!

HELEN.

Explain, among other things, that I've yielded to the desire of the family ——

THADDEUS.

Desire —— ?

HELEN.

That I should accept a share of my father's property.

THADDEUS.

[*Falteringly.*] Thank you—thank you ——

HELEN.

[*After a while.*] That's all, I think.

THADDEUS.

[*Offering his hand to her.*] I—I wish you every happiness, Miss Thornhill. [*She places her hand in his.*] I—I wish you every happiness.

> [*She inclines her head in acknowledgment and again he goes to the door; and again, turning away to the round table where she trifles with a book, she calls him.*

HELEN.

Oh, Mr. Tad —— [*He halts.*] Mr. Tad, I propose that we allow six months to pass in complete silence—six months from to-day ——

THADDEUS.

[*Dully, not understanding.*] Six months—silence ——?

HELEN.

I mean, without my hearing from your wife. Then, perhaps, she—she will send me another invitation ——

THADDEUS.

[*Leaving the door, staring at her.*] Invitation ——?

HELEN.

By that time, we shall, all of us, have forgotten a great deal—sha'n't we? [*Facing him.*] You'll say that to her for me?

> [*He hesitates, then he takes her hands and, bending over them, kisses them repeatedly.*

THADDEUS.

**God** bless you. God bless you. God bless you.

HELEN.

[*Withdrawing her hands.*] Find—Kate ——
[*Once more he makes for the door.*

THADDEUS

[*Stopping half-way and pulling himself together.*] Miss Thornhill—my wife—my wife—you've seen her at a disadvantage—a terrible disadvantage. Few—few pass through life without being seen—once—or oftener—at a disadvantage. She—she's a splendid woman—a splendid woman—a splendid wife and mother. [*Moving to the door.*] They haven't appreciated her—the family haven't appreciated her. They've treated her abominably ; for sixteen years she's been treated abominably. [*At the door.*] But I've never regretted my marriage—[*defiantly*] I've never regretted it—never, for a single moment—never regretted it—never—never regretted it ——
[*He disappears. She goes to the table at the end of the piano and takes up her drawing-block and box of crayons. As she does so,* TRIST *lets himself into the garden. She pauses, listening, and presently he enters the room at the open window.*

TRIST.

[*Throwing his hat on the round table.*] Ah —— !

HELEN.

[*Animatedly.*] Mr. Trist ——

TRIST.

**Yes ?**

HELEN.

Run out to the post-office for me—send a telegram in
my name ——

TRIST.

With pleasure.

HELEN.

Gregory's Hotel, Norfolk Street, Strand, London—the
manager.  Miss Thornhill will arrive to-night—prepare
her room ——

TRIST.

[*His face falling.*]  To-night!

HELEN.

I've altered my plans.  Gregory's Hotel—Gregory's ——

TRIST.

[*Picking up his hat.*]  Norfolk Street, Strand ——

HELEN.

[*At the door.*]  Mr. Trist—I want you to know—I—I've
come into a small fortune.

TRIST.

A fortune ——?

HELEN.

Nearly thirty thousand pounds.

TRIST.

Thirty thousand——!

HELEN.

They've persuaded me—persuaded me to take a share
of my poor father's money.

TRIST.

I—I'm glad.

HELEN.

You—you think I'm doing rightly?

TRIST.

[*Depressed.*]  Why—of course.
> [*She opens the door and he goes to the window.*

HELEN.

Mr. Trist ——— ! [*She comes back into the room.*] Mr. Trist ——— ! [*He approaches her.*]  Mr. Trist—don't—don't ———

TRIST.

What?

HELEN.

[*Her head drooping.*]  Don't let this make any difference between us—will you ——— ?
> [*She raises her eyes to his and they stand looking at each other in silence. Then she turns away abruptly and leaves the room as he hurries through the garden.*

**THE END**

www.ingramcontent.com/pod-product-compliance
Lightning Source LLC
Chambersburg PA
CBHW050512260626
47157CB00004B/1291